HUNTERS
of
Chaos

THE CIRCLE OF LIES

**DON'T MISS ANY
OF THE EXCITEMENT!**

Hunters of Chaos

HUNTERS of Chaos

THE CIRCLE OF LIES

By Crystal Velasquez

ALADDIN

New York   London   Toronto   Sydney   New Delhi

ALADDIN

An imprint of Simon & Schuster Children's Publishing Division

1230 Avenue of the Americas, New York, New York 10020

First Aladdin paperback edition December 2016

Text copyright © 2016 by Working Partners Ltd.

Cover illustration copyright © 2016 by Wylie Beckert

Also available in an Aladdin hardcover edition.

All rights reserved, including the right of reproduction in whole or in part in any form.

ALADDIN is a trademark of Simon & Schuster, Inc., and related logo is a registered trademark of Simon & Schuster, Inc.

For information about special discounts for bulk purchases, please contact Simon & Schuster Special Sales at 1-866-506-1949 or business@simonandschuster.com.

The Simon & Schuster Speakers Bureau can bring authors to your live event. For more information or to book an event contact the Simon & Schuster Speakers Bureau at 1-866-248-3049 or visit our website at www.simonspeakers.com.

Book designed by Laura Lyn DiSiena

The text of this book was set in Warnock Pro.

Manufactured in the United States of America 1116 OFF

2 4 6 8 10 9 7 5 3 1

The Library of Congress has cataloged the hardcover edition as follows:

Velasquez, Crystal, author.

The circle of lies / by Crystal Velasquez.—First Aladdin hardcover edition.

pages cm.—(Hunters of Chaos ; [2])

Summary: "Ana, Doli, Shani, and Lin must continue to battle the forces of the Brotherhood of Chaos and prevent them from taking over the world. However, with Shani expelled from school and living in Mumbai with her father, the four Wildcats have been separated and their power diminished. Can they find a way to stop Anubis this time?"—Provided by publisher.

[1. Shapeshifting—Fiction. 2. Demonology—Fiction. 3. Good and evil—Fiction.]

I. Title. PZ7.V4877Cir 2016

[Fic]—dc23

2015016077

ISBN 978-1-4814-2455-4 (hc)

ISBN 978-1-4814-2456-1 (pbk)

ISBN 978-1-4814-2457-8 (eBook)

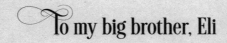

To my big brother, Eli

chapter 1

Ana

WE FILED OUT OF THE DORMS AND MADE OUR WAY TO THE auditorium for school assembly at eight thirty that morning, grumbling about having to get up so early. The sky was its usual shade of cloudless blue. All around us I could see the distant red mountains overlooking Temple Academy like stone guardians.

Nothing had changed—except that the day before, my whole world had fallen apart.

Thankfully, I had three friends who were doing their best to help me put it back together: Doli Hoskie, Lin Yang, and Shani Massri. When I'd first arrived at this school, I hadn't been sure I'd ever fit in. Then I met them, and everything changed. We're all so different from one another, but thanks to Ms. Benitez, we found out that we have one huge thing in common: We are the direct descendants of ancient shape-shifting warriors— Wildcats—who were destined to fight the forces of evil.

I know, that sounds crazy. If I hadn't seen Doli turn into a puma, Lin become a tiger, and Shani transform into a lion—and if I hadn't turned into a jaguar myself—I might not believe it. But after we battled the ancient Egyptian god Anubis and the Chaos Spirits he released, there was no denying the truth. Anyway, I'm getting ahead of myself.

Last night I'd gotten a superweird call from Aunt Teppy. I was starting to suspect that something terrible had happened to her and Uncle Mec, and all I wanted was my family back.

"Tell me one more time what your aunt said," Doli whispered now, pulling us to the side of the entrance to the auditorium. She was looking at me with wide, serious brown eyes, and I realized that I must have looked totally shaken.

I took a deep breath. "She said that they had taken care of me for a decade and they were entitled to some alone time. That I should grow up and look after myself." My voice broke. The words were so upsetting, so unlike my loving aunt, it was still hard to repeat them without crying.

"Harsh," Shani said sympathetically, touching my shoulder. "And then she said that they were in Cancún and not to come looking for them?"

I nodded, feeling a lump forming in my throat. Aunt Teppy and Uncle Mec had always assured me that adopting me after my parents had died had been the best decision they'd ever made. Thinking—for even a moment—that I'd been nothing but a burden to them broke my heart. My only hope was that someone, or some*thing*, had forced her to say it—though the thought of my family in danger scared me even more. "Anubis is behind this; I know it. Aunt Teppy was lying because she had to, or was made to," I said, then added softly, "She had to be."

Anubis, the ancient Egyptian god of the afterlife, was the head of the Brotherhood of Chaos. A collaboration between different ancient civilizations, the Brotherhood had one goal: to cause chaos, both in the ancient world and, now that Anubis was reviving the Brotherhood, in *our* world. Our role as Wildcats was to defeat him.

Unfortunately, he was a very powerful enemy.

Shani pulled out her phone and started typing and clicking. "Well," she said after a moment, "maybe she was lying about the whole alone-time thing, but they really were on a flight to Cancún two days ago." She held up her phone and showed me what looked like an airline passenger list. About a third of the way down were two very familiar names: *Mecatl and Tepin Navarro*.

I gasped and reached for the phone, as if just holding something with their names on it would bring them closer to me. "There they are!" I shouted. But too soon my excitement faded and gave way to a cold fear that seemed to coat my skin like frost. Yes, they had definitely been on the plane, but *why*? I didn't care what my aunt had said on that call. I knew they would never get on a flight without telling me. Which meant they hadn't had a choice.

"How did you get that list?" Doli asked Shani.

"How do you think?" Shani said, giving her a sly look.

Doli groaned. "You hacked into the airline's server?"

Shani looked around with wide eyes at the students and teachers still streaming into the auditorium. "Gosh, Doli. Say it a little louder, why don't you?"

"Sorry. But, Shani, you know you can't afford to get in trouble for hacking again. Were you careful?"

Shani lifted her arm and combed her hand through the patch of blue hair over her left eye. "Look, boss lady, I can either be careful or I can be fast. This time I chose fast, which I'm guessing Ana doesn't have a problem with."

"You're right," I said, hugging her. "Thank you for doing that. You're a good friend." Shani had been kicked out of some other schools—according to the rumor mill it was something like eight or nine—for hacking, among other minor cyber crimes. Principal Ferris had already warned her that if she made one more misstep, she'd be out of Temple Academy, too. It touched me that Shani, who always tried to play it cool when it came to emotional stuff, cared enough about me to take such a huge risk.

Shani hugged me back for a moment and then shook me off. "All right, all right. No need to get mushy. I want to help you find your aunt and uncle, but that's not the only reason

I'm doing this. If their disappearance has anything to do with the Brotherhood of Chaos, then that affects all of us."

Lin and Doli fell silent at the mere mention of the Brotherhood. I knew it was on their minds too.

"You're right again," I said. "Wow, twice in one day. You're on a roll."

Shani began to laugh, but when her eyes caught something behind me, her expression darkened. I turned around to see Coach Lawson approaching, staring down at the smartphone she was holding. Just as she was about to pass us, she glanced up and made eye contact with Shani.

"Miss Massri, how are you this morning?"

Shani stretched her lips into a tight smile. "I'm fantastic, Coach Lawson. And yourself?"

"Wonderful, actually," she said. "My sister had a baby last night, and she just posted some pictures on Facebook. Would you like to see?"

Shani's eyes lit up, and she clapped her hands together. "Would I?"

As Shani took the phone from Coach Lawson and cooed over the pictures of the new baby, Lin, Doli, and I exchanged puzzled looks. I didn't need our Wildcat telepathic powers to know we were all thinking the same thing: *What the heck is going on here?* Shani wasn't exactly the warm and fuzzy type who went all gooey over pictures of puppies and babies.

After a few minutes Shani handed the phone back to

Coach Lawson and said, "Congratulations. She's adorable."

Beaming, Coach Lawson took her phone back. "Thank you." Then after a brief pause, she said, "You know, Miss Massri, I'm sorry you didn't make the tennis team this time. But with a little practice—"

"Yeah, thanks," Shani said, bobbing her head up and down. "You're so right. I'll keep that in mind."

"I hope so," she answered. "The team could use someone with your . . . fire." She turned to all of us. "You'd better get to your seats, ladies. The assembly will be starting soon."

The second she turned to go inside, Lin swung her incredulous gaze to Shani and said, "What in the world—"

"Hold that thought," Shani interrupted, pulling out her own cell phone and pressing a series of buttons. A few seconds later Coach Lawson cried out.

"Oh no! My phone just went black."

"Weird," Shani called. "Must be some sort of power surge. That's been happening a lot lately, since the earthquake. Try turning it off and on again!"

"All right," Coach mumbled, her brows furrowed in concern. "I'll try that." She walked away, shaking her phone as if attempting to wake it from a deep sleep.

When she had gone, Doli crossed her arms and raised one eyebrow at Shani.

"What?" Shani said, her smirk fading as she noticed Doli's glare.

"You did something weird to her phone, didn't you?"

"Who, me?" Shani pointed a finger at her chest, the picture of innocence. But we all knew her too well for that now. "All right, fine. Yes, but she deserved it."

"Why?" I asked. "Because she wouldn't let you on the tennis team? Since when do you even play tennis?"

"I don't. I just figured it would be an easy PE credit. But she blew that for me, so now I have no choice but to take weight training with Coach Hyung, and I'm pretty sure he used to be some sort of drill sergeant in the marines. For that, Coach Lawson must pay." She drummed the tips of her fingers against one another and let out an exaggerated supervillain laugh. *"Mwah-ha-ha-haaa."*

"You know there's another option, right?" Doli cut in, her voice sharp. "You could try to be mature and show a little good sportsmanship instead of killing the poor woman's phone."

"Yeah," Lin added, raising an eyebrow. "Or just *try out again next time*, like the woman said."

Shani scowled. "I could. But where's the fun in that? Besides, I didn't *kill* her phone. I simply installed a virus that'll prevent her from using Facebook's mobile app. Annoying, but not exactly techno-cide. Plus, she's the one who committed an act of attempted murder first. She tried to bore me to death with pictures of that baby." Shani closed her eyes, hung her head to the side, and let her tongue loll out of her mouth.

I bit back a laugh, earning me an annoyed look from Doli

that said, *Don't encourage her!* But I couldn't help it. Even when Shani was being downright wicked, she still cracked me up. Meanwhile, Lin, who had suffered the consequences of Shani's phone hacking in the not-too-distant past, just shrugged and said, "Better her than me."

Finally, we followed the last of the students into the auditorium. Doli hung back with me and whispered, "Let's talk about your aunt and uncle after classes. We're going to find them, okay?"

She squeezed my hand, and I nodded gratefully, trying my best to ignore the worry gnawing at my insides. I knew my friends would do everything in their power—including use their magic—to help me find my family. But for now we had to get through the school day and pretend that we were just normal kids, without a care in the world.

As soon as we settled into our seats, I groaned. My former roommate, Nicole Van Voorhies, was sitting a few rows away, and I could tell that the Wildcats weren't the only ones trying to act normal. Nicole sat at the center of a fawning group of girls. She was twisting a strand of her golden blond hair around her finger and laughing at something Tammy Winston had said. But her eyes were empty, and the rehearsed way she tilted her head back and pumped her shoulders told me that her laugh was just for show. Now that I knew Nicole was actually half-demon, the sound sent chills along my spine.

"Looks like she's recovered nicely from our run-in the other night," Lin said, following my gaze.

"Probably because she was too much of a coward to face us in the temple," I replied.

I shivered again. Everyone had thought that the temple on the far side of the campus that had been revealed after the earthquake was a Native American structure, a relic of the anicent pueblo peoples. But when we'd gotten inside a few nights ago, we'd realized it actually served as the headquarters of the Brotherhood of Chaos. It had become the site of our first battle when a Chaos Spirit in the form of a giant bat had attacked us and brought to life the nightmarish paintings on the temple walls.

If it hadn't been for all of us working together in our Wildcat guises to trap the bat under the heavy statue of Anubis, we wouldn't have made it out of the temple alive.

Outside the temple we'd caught Nicole skulking around, spying for Anubis. It turned out Nicole wasn't quite human. Whereas we were girls who could turn into Wildcats, Nicole was more hyena than girl.

"I can't even believe she's here," I whispered to Lin. "Shouldn't she be off somewhere with Anubis, wreaking havoc?"

Lin narrowed her eyes at Nicole and said, "She probably wants to lie low for a while after the way we totally ran her boss out of town. I doubt she's brave enough to do anything on her own."

That much was true. Nicole had never attacked me when we'd been alone together. Not physically, anyway. But the thing about hyenas was that they hunted in packs. Or so *The Lion King* had taught me. "Do you think she was serious when she said there were more like her at the school?"

But Lin just shrugged it off. "So what if there are?" she said. "Even in the wild, hyenas would be no match for a lion, a tiger, a puma, and a jaguar. If they're smart, they'll keep their distance."

She had a point, but the thought of a half-demon hyena posse sitting all around us still gave me the creeps. And besides, no one had ever accused Nicole of being smart.

"Good morning, students and faculty," Principal Ferris said, stepping up to the podium onstage.

Everyone quieted down and muttered a sluggish "Good morning" back. Usually she would say something like, *You can do better than that* and make us say it again. But today she looked distracted. "I'm afraid I have some rather upsetting news to share. It seems that over the weekend there was some sort of . . . event at the temple."

Shani and I looked at each other. "About time," she whispered. The battle in the temple had taken place days ago, and we'd been expecting an announcement like this ever since.

"We are not yet sure if it was an act of vandalism or the result of minor aftershocks, but several of the priceless artifacts that were excavated have been damaged. In addition . . ." Here

Principal Ferris's voice trailed off as she paused and took out a piece of paper from her pocket. She looked at it and shook her head sadly as if the paper itself had broken her heart. "Dr. Logan has written a letter informing me that he's left Temple Academy to pursue a project in Zimbabwe. He . . . he won't be returning."

At this last bit of news, the room began to buzz with conversation. Jessica, who had a not-so-secret crush on Dr. Logan, cried out, "No!" Of course, I doubted she would have been quite as upset if she'd seen Dr. Logan in his true half-man, half-jackal form, his perfect white teeth and neat hair replaced by jagged fangs and matted fur. "Dr. Logan" was just the human form Anubis had taken to get onto school grounds.

Principal Ferris folded the note and slipped it back into her pocket. "As a result of these developments, the temple itself has been sealed, and the historical foundation has halted any further exploration for the time being. This means that the plans to relocate Temple Academy have also been canceled."

This time everyone cheered and applauded. No one had wanted the school to move—not the teachers and not the students—so this was great news for them. As for Lin, Doli, Shani, and me, we cheered because we had succeeded in ruining Anubis's plan to take over the campus and use the temple for his own sinister purposes. In fact, the only person who didn't seem thrilled by the news was Principal Ferris.

Shani leaned over and whispered, "By my count, that makes Hunters of Chaos two; Anubis a big fat zero."

Principal Ferris moved on to less exciting announcements, and then the choir got up to sing the national anthem. Finally the assembly came to a close. Doli stood and said, "Let's hurry. We have to squeeze in our appointment with Ms. Benitez before class."

I rose to follow her, but then I saw Jason Ferris standing near the back of the auditorium. "Ferris" as in Principal Ferris's son. What was he doing here? "Uh, I'll meet you outside," I said. "I'll just be a sec."

Doli followed my gaze to Jason and snickered. "Fine."

Shani shrugged, and my friends disappeared into the cluster of students leaving the auditorium. Only when I saw them exit the room did I sidle up next to Jason and say, "Hey."

Jason turned to face me, and for a second I forgot how to breathe. Sure, those incredible blue-green eyes and that dirty-blond hair streaked with gold made him seriously cute. But now I also knew how brave, kind, and selfless he was. He'd risked his life in the temple to help us defeat the bat Chaos Spirit. As far as I was concerned, Harry Styles had nothing on Jason Ferris.

"H-hey, Ana," he stammered, giving me an awkward hug.

"Were you waiting for me?" I asked when I pulled away.

"Well, yeah. I, um . . ." He bowed his head, then scratched the back of it, peeking up at me so only a hint of blue showed beneath his long eyelashes. "I just wanted to ask you, you know, how you are."

"Oh, uh, I'm okay, I guess." I twisted my fingers together behind my back, urging myself to be cool. "How are you?"

"Good. Good," he said. "How are you?"

I giggled and bit my lip. "You already asked me that."

"I did?" he said, his eyes widening. He stared down at his sneakers. "Oh yeah, I guess I did." He winced and smacked his forehead, whispering, "Stupid, stupid, stupid" to himself.

I laughed and grabbed his hand. "Hey, that's my friend you're hitting," I said.

He let out a shuddering sigh, looking at our joined hands and then up at me with a half smile. "Sorry I'm being such a dork. It's just—it's really good to see you."

I nodded, feeling my stomach tingle. "It's good to see you, too. It's nice to have something to think about besides my aunt and uncle."

Jason's eyes darkened with concern, and he moved closer to me. Doli had called him the night before to let him know about the phone call. "Has there been any news since last night?"

I shook my head. "We're working on it. We're actually on our way to see Ms. Benitez now, if you want to come with us."

"I would," he said, "but I should really go check on my mom."

We both glanced toward the stage and saw Principal Ferris just standing there with a faraway look in her eye.

"She seems kind of down," I noted. "Is everything all right?"

Jason sighed and shook his head. "Believe it or not, I think she's just missing that creep Dr. Logan. She carries that note around with her all the time. I've caught her taking it out to read every once in a while, like she's hoping this time it'll say something different. I wish I could tell her he was actually a force of ancient evil so she would get over him, but she still thinks he was a stand-up guy. How messed up is that?"

"Pretty messed up," I agreed, "but it's not her fault. He had weird power over some people. But now that he's gone, maybe she'll get over him."

"I hope so," Jason said. "I really want her to be as happy as I am." He squeezed my hand and gave me a shy smile before walking away. How could I feel so good about Jason, I wondered, and so bad about everything else at the same time?

Outside, Shani, Lin, and Doli were waiting for me.

"Sooo . . . how's Jason?" Doli asked with a knowing smile.

I felt my face warm. No use trying to deny it. "He's fine."

"Then why do you look so confused?" Lin asked.

"Because boys are confusing," Shani answered for me. "And relationships are already hard enough without your crush knowing that you're an evil-fighting wildcat who occasionally turns into a jaguar."

We all burst into laughter. It was funny because it was true.

In the morning light cascading through her office window, Ms. Benitez looked a little faded, like a beloved T-shirt that had been washed one too many times. She had been out of the hospital for a few days now and had nearly recovered from Anubis's attack. But she was clearly still weak. In her current state no one would ever suspect that she was really Ixchel, a Mayan goddess of war who'd been battling Anubis for centuries. The plain-looking history teacher with the dark brown eyes and hair, and eyeglasses hanging from a chain around her neck, was just a disguise she wore while she secretly helped to keep legendary evils at bay. In her real form, Ixchel was not someone you wanted to tangle with.

Thankfully, she was on our side.

"Girls!" she said when we walked in. She lifted her thin arms. "Wonderful to see you."

I noticed that she remained in her chair behind the desk instead of standing to greet us.

"Good to see you, too," Doli replied, leaning against the wall. "How are you feeling? Will you be back in class soon?"

"I hope so, but I'd like to be at my full strength. Principal Ferris is generously allowing me to ease my way back in. I've told her that my weakness is a result of pain medications my doctor prescribed. She's been very understanding." She paused, taking time to look at each of us carefully. "But I'm much more concerned about all of you. Are you all right?"

"No," I said immediately. I took a seat across from her desk. "No, I'm not." Maybe because I'd tried so hard to shove my feelings down all morning, or maybe because Ms. Benitez was looking at me in the same caring way that Aunt Teppy usually did, I started to cry.

Doli filled Ms. Benitez in about the awful phone call with my aunt, while Lin found a handful of tissues for me.

"All we know for sure," Shani added, "is that they flew to Cancún two days ago."

"Please don't ask us how we know that," said Doli, shooting Shani a look.

Ms. Benitez's color grew even paler. She rose from her seat behind the desk, walked over to her window, and grasped the sill for support. "Ana, I can't deny—I'm troubled by this. Since your aunt and uncle donated the original vase that imprisoned the Chaos Spirits, I have to wonder if they know about the Brotherhood of Chaos."

I shook my head, dabbing the tears away from my cheek. Once I'd gotten to Temple, I'd found out that my aunt and uncle had donated a very valuable Mayan vase decorated with stylized cat figures. It was through the destruction of the vase that we'd gotten our powers. "I don't know," I said honestly. "I didn't even know they owned that vase until you told us. Of course, they also didn't tell me until I enrolled that my parents had met here, so it's possible they have other secrets."

Ms. Benitez nodded and made a humming sound deep in her throat. "I must tell you that Cancún is a place the Brotherhood would be drawn to."

"You mean . . . my aunt and uncle might have been brought there for a reason?" I asked. "Something involving Anubis?"

"It's possible. If they were forced to go there, Anubis may be using them as bait to lure you to a place where the magical scales could be tipped in his favor."

"Really? Cancún? I thought that town was just full of sweaty beaches and college kids," Lin said.

"Yes." Ms. Benitez nodded patiently. "Beaches, college kids, and ancient ruins of temples that house enormous sources of magical power."

Oh, Lin mouthed silently.

Ms. Benitez turned to me. She seemed to be struggling to choose the right words. "Whether your aunt and uncle went to Cancún by choice or by force," she said, "they could be in real danger."

I felt a swift rush of fear whip through me, making my palms sweat and my breath come short. If even Ms. Benitez thought my aunt and uncle were in trouble, then it wasn't all in my head. If anything happened to them . . . No, I couldn't think about that. I had to focus on helping them, but how? *"What do I do?"* I cried desperately.

She stood in front of my chair, and I watched as her eyes took on that mystical plum color that belonged to Ixchel. "You do nothing," she said. "I will go to Cancún. I have contacts there who can help me find them."

I breathed out a sigh of relief, feeling some of the tension in my shoulders ease. "When can you go? I know this is a lot to ask, but I'm so worried, and with everything that's going on, I just—"

Ixchel placed her hand over mine, and I felt a soft pulse of soothing energy flow into me, like a cup of warm tea. "I will go tonight," she said. "I'm sure Shani can assist me in booking a ticket."

Shani pulled her phone out of her pocket and started tapping away. "Consider it done."

chapter 2

Ana

AT NIGHT I PACE BEHIND THE GLASS WALL OF A ZOO enclosure, watching the people come and go on the other side of the barrier. Uncle Mec and Aunt Teppy show up. Uncle Mec holds four colorful helium balloons that float high above his head, and Aunt Teppy is happily eating pink cotton candy and pointing at all the big cats. I try calling out to them, but they don't recognize me, and right behind them stands a man in a cream-colored linen suit, flashing a grin full of jagged teeth—Anubis. It was just as I roared and threw myself against the glass, trying in vain to break through, that a shrill ringing ripped me from my dream.

It took a second for my breathing to slow. *It wasn't real*, I told myself, reaching for my phone, which was still ringing. *It was just a dream.* But I knew I wouldn't be able to shake it off that easily.

Across the room Lin shifted in her sleep and mumbled something but didn't wake up. The alarm clock on my desk read 1:15 a.m.

Who would be calling me at this time of night?

I reached into my backpack and pulled out my cell phone to see a number I didn't recognize. Could it be Ms. Benitez calling from Cancún to tell me she had found my aunt and uncle? I fumbled to unlock the phone and hit the answer key.

"Hello? Ms. Benitez? Did you find them?"

"This is your aunt, Ana."

"Aunt Teppy?" I cried, suddenly fully awake. "Where are you? Are you all right?"

"I'd be better if you would just leave me alone already," she said.

I felt my heart squeeze. She sounded furious, though there was a weird quiver in her voice that I didn't recognize. "Aunt Teppy, what are you talking about?"

"If you want to know, come meet me in the gazebo right now, young lady. We can settle this once and for all." She let out a weird giggle. Was this some kind of joke to her?

"Did you say the gazebo? Does that mean you're here, at the school?"

"Obviously, genius. Stop asking questions and come outside. I don't have all night."

When the line went dead, I realized I was shaking. I didn't know what was going on, but I had to find out. I leaped from my bed, opened the closet, and threw on some clothes. By the time I was tying the laces on my sneakers, Lin's eyes had fluttered open. "Where are you going?" she asked. "Don't tell me the cat wants you to go on another midnight adventure."

I shook my head, my eyes flicking toward the soft black bundle on Lin's duvet. The stray cat had more or less adopted us after leading us to our battle in the temple. "No, the cat's asleep at the foot of your bed. My aunt just called."

Lin sat up, reached for her desk lamp, and flipped it on. She squinted against the light. "What? So Ms. Benitez found her? Did she say anything about the Brotherhood? Is she all right? Is your uncle with her?"

"I don't know," I told her. "But she's here. She just told me to meet her in the gazebo."

"Here?" Lin repeated. "Like, *here* here? How can that be?"

"I don't know!" I repeated, frustrated that I didn't have any answers. "All I know is she wants to meet me right now, so I'm going."

"Not by yourself, you aren't," Lin said wearily. She threw back her covers and went to the closet to get dressed.

I wanted to tell her she didn't have to come, that I would be fine on my own. But the truth was, I wanted her with me. The way Aunt Teppy had sounded on the phone told me something wasn't right. In fact, I was worried that something was very, very wrong.

On our way out, Lin rapped on the door to Shani and Doli's room.

"What are you doing?" I asked. "We don't have to ruin

their night too." I felt bad enough that I had dragged Lin into my drama.

"Yes, we do," Lin said. "We're a team, remember? We're stronger together."

A wave of gratitude washed over me. It felt good to know I wasn't alone. "Thanks, Lin," I whispered. "Remind me to hug you later."

A few seconds later a bleary-eyed Shani opened the door. When she saw Lin, she huffed and said, "This had better be good, Yang."

Ten minutes later all four of us sneaked out of the dorm and headed for the gazebo, shivering in the cold.

"Why would she want you to meet her here?" Doli asked once we were outside.

"Beats me. Maybe going inside the dorms where my mom used to live would've been too hard for her. Maybe she's been short with me lately because my going to Temple brings up painful memories."

Shani jumped onto a bench we were passing and leaped down again, almost as gracefully as she would have in her lion form. "I don't know, Ana. Look"—she pointed at the small wooden frame next to the tennis courts that overlooked the woods—"the gazebo's empty."

As I followed her gaze, my stomach lurched. As frightened as I'd been about seeing Aunt Teppy under Anubis's control, it was even worse not to see her at all. I bent forward with my hands on my knees. "I think I'm going to be sick."

"Don't worry, Ana," Doli said, rushing to my side and stroking my back. "We'll keep a look—" She broke off so abruptly that I peered up at her. She was gazing at a point off in the distance. "There—there are lights on in the gym," she said.

"What?" I looked beyond the tennis courts and saw the bright yellow light filling the gym windows. I stood up straight. "Maybe she got cold and went in there to warm up?"

"Only one way to find out," said Shani.

"This is officially spooky," Lin whined. "Who votes we go home right now?" She raised her hand high in the air.

But Doli was already leading the way to the gym at a slow jog, with Shani following close behind. I grabbed Lin's other hand and said, "Stronger together, right?" She groaned but matched my pace. Soon we were just outside the gym.

"It might not be her in there," Doli said. "It could be a teacher, for all we know. So let's sneak in through the side door. At least that way whoever's in there won't see us right away."

"Sounds like a plan, boss lady," said Shani.

"Would you stop calling me that?" Doli whispered.

"Nope. But don't worry, I mean it in a good way."

We tiptoed around to the side entrance of the gym, which thankfully was unlocked. We gave one another a last glance before we crept inside, single file. I'm not sure what I was hoping to see, but except for the sports equipment stacked neatly at the back of the room and the rack of bleachers against the wall, the gym was as empty as the gazebo.

"What gives?" said Shani. "If your aunt is playing hide-and-seek, she picked a really weird time to do it."

"I don't know what to say," I murmured, walking farther into the open space. "This isn't like her. But then, I don't even understand how she got into Temple in the first place. Isn't the gate locked at night?"

Before anyone had a chance to answer, the lights shut off and we were in total darkness. Someone—Lin, I thought—let out a high-pitched yelp. Seconds later the lights went back on, and I saw Shani standing by the fuse box just outside the gym. "Stupid old building," she grumbled. "You'd think with all the tuition we pay, they could afford to replace the electrical system so we'd have lights that actually worked."

As if the building itself had heard her and were insulted, the lights blinked out again, and this time no amount of messing with the fuse box would turn them back on. With only the moon outside casting its faint glow, the darkness felt suffocating, like someone had thrown a black wool blanket over my head and was squeezing tight. I knew it was panic setting in. Anything could have been coming for us in the dark.

"Okay, I might change my vote now. I'm with Lin. Let's get out of here," said Shani's voice.

But it was too late. As my eyes adjusted to the dark, I

glimpsed something swooping out of the blackness, aiming right for us. At first it seemed like a flying strip of gauze, as transparent as a ghost. As it got closer, the figure took on form and shape, becoming all too real. "Something's there!" I shouted, frantically searching the room to find it again.

Just when I thought I'd spotted it, it circled around and slipped into the shadows.

"Where? Where?" Doli yelled. She bumped up next to me so that we were back-to-back. Only then did I realize that my back was soaked in a cold sweat.

"I can't see anything," Lin said, reaching out for us. Shani followed her, and the four of us stood shoulder-to-shoulder, each facing a different direction.

"Me neither," Shani said. "Are you sure you saw something, Ana?"

"Positive," I said. "At least I think so. . . ." I started to doubt myself, until a second later a large bird zoomed out of the rafters and sailed toward us, its eyes burning with a malevolent fire and its wings sending an eerie whistle through the air. "Watch out!" I screamed, trying to drag the other girls to the floor by their shirts. I ducked, but the bird's razor-sharp talons tore into my shoulder.

I cried out in pain as it soared up to the vaulted ceiling, spreading its enormous wings. It circled in place and shot straight down with an unearthly shriek. I screamed again, but this time it came out as a roar. Without even realizing it, I had started to transform into my jaguar self. I felt that familiar shimmer of magic tingling through my body as my legs lengthened and stretched, turning into muscular haunches covered in blond fur. The thumping in my chest doubled its rhythm as my human heart became that of a Wildcat. My tongue grew long and heavy in my mouth while my teeth lengthened into sharp points, meant for killing. The transformation was painless, but with it came a lust for blood so strong, it was almost frightening.

With my cat eyes I focused on the shadowy figure speeding toward me. Its hard yellow beak opened wide, and its yellow eyes, bulging like glittering marbles, burned into me mercilessly. This was no ordinary bird, I realized—it was a bald eagle, one of the most dangerous predators in the wild. My mind flashed back to the night the vase was destroyed in the basement of the museum, releasing the four Chaos Spirits. Suddenly the truth of what was happening slapped me in the face. That night in the museum basement weeks ago when we first saw the Chaos Spirits, there had been a bat, a monkey, a snake, and . . . an eagle! *This eagle isn't real,* I realized with a jolt. *It's a Chaos Spirit, and we're under attack!*

Where is my aunt? I hadn't seen any sign of her. Had this all been just a setup to get us alone, where no one could hear us cry for help?

You guys, it's a Chaos Spirit! I called, but they were still in their human guises and couldn't hear me. We could communicate telepathically only as cats. Just before the bird reached me, I dived out of the way, barreling into Lin and Doli, who screeched in pain. I knew the enormous weight of my jaguar body was crushing them. I struggled to my paws, leaped into the air, and slashed at the bird, which had somehow multiplied. Had it turned into two birds? Three? It was hard to tell as they swooped in again and again, their talons ripping into my skin. I could taste blood, and I had the sinking feeling that it was mine.

"I'm getting these lights on *now*!" Shani yelled. "Maybe it'll scare them off." She raced for the fuse box in the hall again. Even from way across the room, with my cat senses I could hear every one of Shani's frantic breaths and smell the sour scent of fear seeping from her pores.

"I'll move the bleachers. We can hide underneath!" Doli called, getting to her feet and running for the stacks. But the bleachers were heavy and the wheels were locked in place. No matter how hard she pushed, they wouldn't budge. Finally she gave up, reached for the row of basketballs, and started hurling them at the birds. Most of the balls sailed right past, but even when they connected, the birds barely slowed down.

Meanwhile, as soon as Lin had gotten free of my weight, she'd rolled away and squeezed her eyes shut. "Tiger, tiger, tiger . . . ," she chanted, balling her hands into fists. Now I understood why she hadn't shifted yet. She was too panicked to focus. As I did my best to shield her from the eagles, I laid one heavy paw on her stomach until she eased her eyes open.

I couldn't talk to her, but I hoped just having her stare into my large round cat eyes would get the message across. *Calm down and let the cat take over.* She blinked slowly and nodded, understanding clear on her face. She took a deep breath. In seconds her delicate hands became the heavy orange-and-white paws of a tiger. Her cat body rippled over her human one like a coat of armor. She let out a satisfied growl and got to her paws, eyeing the birds with a hunter's yearning. *Let's do this,* she said. Together we leaped at the birds, baring our teeth and slashing at the air.

Pull them down so I can bite them, I urged Lin.

I'm trying! she answered. *But they won't stay still. . . .*

I knew what she meant. I felt my claws scrape against their feathers, but before I could get a good grip, they swooped away, just out of reach.

"Got it!" Shani yelled from across the room, and the lights came on all at once. The birds, thrown off by the sudden flash of light, snapped their beaks at us but wheeled around, flapping their dark wings until they had all wrapped their talons around the top level of the bleachers. Their angry screeches echoing around us scraped the inside of my sensitive ears like an ice pick dragging against concrete. But they had backed off long enough for me to take a good look around.

What I saw almost made me wish they hadn't.

Temple Academy's sports teams were all called the Fighting Eagles, and the mascot, Eddie the Eagle, smiled out from each of the banners hung beneath the scoreboards and from the mural on the wall. He looked out from a logo stamped onto each of the basketballs that now lay strewn around the gym floor. Or at least, he had. Now the cartoon eagle mascot was missing from half of the banners and all of the basketballs, and while he usually wore a friendly grin, the remaining images of him leered at us with menacing eyes. The large white heads on the banners swung from left to right as if they were trying to wriggle free. Atop the scoreboard perched two eagles, preening their feathers. *This can't be happening,* I thought, fighting the instinct to run.

Doli let out a bloodcurdling scream, and I swung my head in her direction. She was staring down at her track team T-shirt, which of course had an eagle in the center. But now the eagle was coming to life right before our eyes. Lin roared, and it seemed to remind Doli what she had to do.

In seconds her dark skin had been replaced with thick sandy fur, her tall runner's body reshaping itself into a powerful puma. Her eyes glowed yellow, and she growled, pouncing on the eagle that had been trying to rip out her hair.

Shani ran to help. As she did, her blue-and-black hair and red-shale-colored skin gave way to the golden fur of a lion, and her roar shook the windows in their frames.

In answer the eagles watching balefully from the scoreboard lifted their wings, at least six feet across, and dive-bombed us like missiles. I barely had time to react before one of the birds landed on my back, sinking its talons into my fur and squeezing with all its might. It felt like someone was pinching my skin with a pair of hot pliers. *"GAAAAR!"* I roared. I tried to twist my head to bite at the eagle, but its beak pecked at my eyes, trying to blind me.

I backed toward a wall and reared up on my hind legs, crushing the great bird against the wall with my body. It screamed in protest, but then I heard its bones shatter against my back like broken plates. When I fell onto my front paws again, the eagle's limp body came with me. Its talons were still lodged in my flesh. *Help!* I called, burning with pain.

I'm coming, Shani said. Soon she was at my side, panting heavily.

We'll distract the birds while you help Ana, said Doli. The sound of flapping wings echoed close by, but we ignored it. *This might hurt,* Shani said. I heard the crunch of her teeth sinking into the dead eagle's body. It took three strong yanks, but she finally pulled it free, leaving my back throbbing.

It might *hurt?* I asked.

Consider yourself lucky, Shani replied. *Eagles aim for your spine so they can sever it with their beaks. Watch out! Here they come again!*

These birds were smart. They came at us all at once and never let up. One clawed and scratched Doli's head, opening up puncture wounds across her skull as if it were trying to gouge her eyes. I bounded toward her, ready to pounce on them, but another bird grabbed my tail in its hard beak and pulled me back. They seemed to be multiplying by the minute. This time we weren't battling a murder of small black crows, like we had in the temple. These were powerful birds of prey, skilled at taking down their enemies, and Jason wasn't here with a lit torch to stave them off.

I could smell the scent of fresh blood filling the room, and I knew it was mostly ours. It poured, thick and red, from a wound on my arm, and tufts of Lin's orange fur stuck out of one of the eagles' beaks, her blood crusting its edges. Confusion ruled, but I was sure of three things:

We were brave.

We were fighting hard.

And we were losing.

chapter 3
Shani

I never liked Eddie the Eagle. As mascots go, he's pretty lame—especially when our school plays against teams with serious animal street cred: wolverines, barracudas, rattlesnakes. I never thought eagles were that level of scary.

Until they started trying to kill us, that is.

Think, Shani, think! I ordered myself. I roared in frustration, baring my teeth at the eagle that kept swooping in to claw at my back. I knew I had a weight advantage, and my claws were just as sharp as its talons. Not to mention I had the whole magical-Hunter-of-Chaos-with-an-ancient-calling thing working for me. The eagle turned and dived, its wings tucked behind it, a missile bearing razor talons and a scythe-like beak. It ducked my flailing paw, and I rolled to the side—but it still pulled out a clump of my hair. Somehow the stupid eagle was kicking my magical butt.

When I turned to see how my friends were matching up

against the other eagles, the one I was fighting flew right at me, landed on my neck, and pecked at my head—coming away with a chunk of my ear in its beak. I felt like my head was on fire, and the roar I let out scared even me. But it wasn't just pain—it was blind animal rage.

I realized I'd been thinking too hard. My lion self would know what to do if I just surrendered to it. I tried putting away my human thoughts and instead pictured myself in a field of tall grass, creeping quietly toward my next meal. I could almost feel the sun warming my fur, hear the gurgling of rivers, smell the fear of the other animals nearby, none wanting to get between me and my prey. Then, when my target least expected it . . .

I pounced. The bird had come in, nice and low, intending to claw my back again, but I had whipped around and leaped at just the right time, my paws crushing the bird's body against the cold gym floor. A strange hunger took over me, and I lowered my head to rip out the eagle's throat.

No sooner was that eagle defeated, though, than another one came flying at me with the same intensity. I jumped back into my fighting stance, realizing with a sick feeling that maybe I wouldn't win this time. With each passing minute the birds seemed to be getting more efficient, and more brutal. For Chaos Spirits, their attacks were becoming eerily organized. One of them flew in low, letting its wings carry it down in an easy glide. When it got within range, it sliced into Lin's back with its blood-soaked steel talons, then flapped just enough to get out of range of her deadly tiger claws. As Lin reared to strike the first bird, a second eagle torpedoed straight down at her and collided with Lin's head at full speed, kamikaze style. At that velocity, its weight knocked Lin to the ground like a wet sandbag, even as the eagle bounced away and landed in a crumpled heap right beside her. Lin didn't move for several seconds, and I thought the bird might have knocked her out cold. But then I heard a pained mewling sound.

This isn't working! Lin's panicked voice streamed into my mind.

There are too many of them. That was Ana. She had bounded to the top of the bleachers, attempting to get at the birds where they were least able to use their speed against her. Smart. But while she bit into one bird's throat, breaking its neck with an audible *snap*, another clamped onto her leg and dragged her toward the edge. It was trying to push her from the top of the stack, the same way they would kill smaller prey by dragging them off a cliff and dropping them onto the jagged rocks below. Ana sank her claws into the wood, scrambling to keep hold and get a grip on the bleachers, but she hadn't expected the bird's powerful tug from behind her.

Ana! I screamed, running to the base of the bleachers just as she went tumbling over the edge. The eagle screeched in triumph, but as Ana fell, her body twisted and positioned itself so that she landed lightly on her feet. Even she seemed surprised.

Ha! The eagle had forgotten. That method might work on goats and deer, but Ana was a cat. We were designed to land on our feet.

My celebration was short-lived. Doli had been quiet all this time because she had been busy fighting off two eagles that had decided to team up against her. While one flew at her face and nipped at her eyelids with its beak, which punctured her skin like a yellow ice pick, the other tore a deep gash down her side, and Doli let out a tortured puma scream. Her coat darkened to a reddish brown as blood seeped from the wound.

I ran to join Doli, but another eagle flew into my path, spreading its enormous wings to the sides as it let out a high-pitched cry that sounded like a car alarm. Its fetid breath reeked of death. I wasted no time—I pounced with lightning quickness and sank my jaws into its soft underbelly. It pecked at my head, drawing blood and bright white points of pain, but I wouldn't let go until it went limp in my mouth. When I had thrown the fallen bird to the side, I looked up to find four more eagles where there had only been one—all of them blocking my path to Doli.

Where were they all coming from? There hadn't been this many of them a minute ago. I looked at the mascot banner and saw eagles pulling themselves out of it. At least a dozen more now lined the bleachers, patiently waiting for their turn to attack.

We'll never beat them like this, I told the girls.

I know, but what can we do? Ana answered. *We're drowning here.*

That's it, I thought suddenly. *Hold them off as long as you can,* I told my friends.

Like we have a choice, Lin grumbled.

I batted my way past the growing swarm of birds and ran for the hallway. All the while I pictured Doli running on the outdoor track with her team, me typing away on my laptop—*people* things, not cat things. By the time I reached the fuse box, I was human again.

But my ear still stung like crazy. I remembered the eagle taking a bite out of my ear and realized that I had carried my injuries with me into my human form. If the same happened to Doli, she was going to need help, and fast.

I shook my head and willed myself to concentrate. I had only a few minutes to get this done. I threw open the main gym door and found the manual crank that controlled all the windows. It took a few tries before I could force the crank around, but slowly the windows angled open. I searched the wall where I'd found the fuse box and finally spotted a small digital screen. "Jackpot," I said with a smile.

As part of all the renovations Temple Academy had done last year, they'd installed tablets in each of the buildings to make it easier for the groundskeepers to control things like the lights and the alarm systems. But I wasn't interested in either of those things at the moment. I quickly signed in as Principal Ferris—I knew hacking her password would come in handy one day—and found the controls for the sprinkler system. Being a lion had its advantages, but the gamechanger was going to be one swipe from my human finger.

Immediately the sprinklers in the gym ceiling opened up and let out a forceful spray, hitting the eagles as if they were flames to be put out. The sprinklers turning on automatically triggered the emergency lights, which—unlike the regular yellow recess lights—were a blinding white meant for maximum clarity.

From my place in the hall I heard the three Wildcats yelp at the same time—probably when that ice-cold water hit them. I would have been sorry if the plan hadn't been working so well. I ran back inside the gym and saw that the eagles waiting their turn on the risers were not nearly as solid as they'd been when I'd left. I could see right through them now. Maybe they had to focus to become solid enough to attack, and the rush of cold water had been startling enough to interrupt the process.

As Anubis's influence seemed to seep out of them, they began to evaporate like steam. The birds abandoned their attack as water soaked into their feathers. Meanwhile, the ones who tried to escape the water blasts by shooting toward the ceiling flew straight into the blinding beams of the emergency lights head-on, which they didn't seem to like at all. It wasn't long before one of them let out a ghastly cry. I don't speak eagle, but I'm guessing what he said was, "Retreat!"

Like in a cartoon stampede, they all headed for the open windows and the door, and streamed into the night. There were so many of them cascading through the windows, the fluorescent light reflecting off their bright white heads over their brown feathers, that the effect was like watching a muddy ocean tide, whitecaps breaking against the shore. If only it were that easy to wash them out to sea.

For several minutes all we could do was listen to the *whoosh, whoosh, whoosh* of their frantic flapping, the tick of their beaks against the windowpanes like pebbles hitting glass, and their insistent outraged shrieks. The ruckus was almost too much to take. All of us whimpered, pawing at our ears.

The moment the eagles were all gone, my friends turned back into the humans I knew, clearly exhausted from the effort it had taken to fight the Chaos Spirits.

"You . . . you did it," Ana panted as she sat heavily on the gym floor, thin rivulets of blood oozing from several puncture wounds on her arms and forehead. "Nice job."

"I definitely owe you one," Lin added. "We all do." Lin's cheek was swollen and bruised, and there was a trail of four long scratches across her neck that disappeared beneath her T-shirt. But she seemed so grateful to be alive that she barely noticed her injuries.

Doli nodded her agreement as I sat down beside her. Even that tiny movement made her grimace.

"Thanks, guys, but why don't we save the applause for after we figure out if Doli is going to need a new spleen or something. If you haven't noticed, she's bleeding all over the place," I said.

Ana knelt in front of Doli then and examined the gash in her side, which was sopping wet with bright red blood that refused to clot. "Doli," Ana said, panic creeping into her voice, "this looks bad. That eagle cut you pretty deep, and the wound is still bleeding."

"It is?" Doli said, straining to see her side. "Mm. That must be why I feel like I'm about to pass out."

Ana glanced up at me, her brown eyes darkening with worry. "We've got to get her to the infirmary."

"Are you crazy?" Lin spoke up. "We can't do that. What would we say? That she got attacked by the school mascot, who came to life thanks to a bunch of Chaos Spirits sent by an evil brotherhood who—?"

"Okay, okay, I get it. When you say it like that, it sounds nuts," I said.

"Lin's right," Doli broke in, pressing her hand into her side and wincing. She shook her head as if to clear away the dizziness. When she spoke again, her voice was firm. "We can't tell anyone about this. Besides, I'm okay. Really. We just have to get back to the dorm. There's a first aid kit in the bathroom cabinet. You're all going to need it too. Especially you, Shani. That ear looks gross."

As the adrenaline that had coursed through me during the fight subsided, I started to feel the effects of every beak strike and talon grip. I reached my hand up and touched my ear, hissing at the pain beginning to throb from the torn lobe. I pulled my hand away and stared at my fingertips. They were covered in blood.

"Hold on." I ran back to the tablet. Soon I had the sprinklers and the emergency lights turned off and the regular recess lights back on. When I returned, I lifted my eyebrows and said, "We need to get the heck out of here now before someone sees us."

I looked at Ana and Lin, at the scratches on their necks and arms, and realized that our dorm mother was bound to ask us how we'd gotten these injuries. "We're all going to have to come up with a creative story to explain the obvious cuts and bruises to Mrs. O'Grady. Something that doesn't involve demented ghost eagles."

But Ana was shaking her head and looking around the gym. "No, we're going to need a way to explain *this*," she said in a defeated tone. "We've completely destroyed the gym!"

We each turned to take in all the damage. The floor was a mess of splintered wood and shattered glass from the windows that some of the eagles had broken on their way out. The walls had huge chunks missing, as if a wrecking ball had smashed into them, and all the basketball nets had been torn down. Not to mention that the water from the sprinklers was now warping the wood so it bulged and sank in uneven waves.

"Ooh, not good, not good, not good," said Lin, stating the obvious. "If I get caught for this, my parents will disown me. Or worse, they'll make me spend the summer with my most distant relatives in China."

"So let's get out of here," I said. "Come on!"

"We're just going to leave it like this?" Ana looked help-lessly around the room.

"We *have* to," I insisted. "Ana, I can't be caught here. I'm already on my last warning. Besides, fixing this damage would take way more than a mop and a broom. Look around."

"But . . . but what about my aunt?" Ana searched the room desperately, tears filling her eyes.

Doli approached, and with her free hand she squeezed Ana's shoulder. "I'm sorry, Ana, but your aunt isn't here. I don't think she ever was. Maybe Anubis made your aunt speak to you on the phone to get you here. It was just one of his tricks."

Ana nodded, her eyes wet with tears. "I know. I guess I just needed to hear that out loud."

I gestured for everyone to move toward the exit and pat-ted Ana on the back. "Look on the bright side," I said. "They took us on and we won—again. We're going to find your aunt and uncle and make the Brotherhood of Chaos wish they had never messed with us."

"Agreed," said Doli. "But for now let's get to the dorm so we can dress these wounds and get some sleep. We're going to need it."

We had just rounded the corner of the tennis courts when we saw an even more unpleasant sight than the killer eagles: Nicole Van Voorhies emerging from the shadows.

"What are you doing here?" I demanded.

"Just taking a walk to clear my head," she replied casually.

"At two in the morning?"

She shrugged. "I couldn't sleep. Besides, all of you are awake too. So what have you been up to? Something that'll get you tossed out of here, I hope," she said with a giggle, taking in our soaking wet clothes and bloody faces. "Have you been swimming after hours?"

I heard Ana gasp, and looked over at her. Her eyes darkened. "That's the same giggle I heard on the phone earlier!" she hissed. "That wasn't my aunt, was it? It was you!"

It took a moment for me to take in what Ana was saying. Then I realized. *Of course!* Nicole was a hyena demon—and hyenas could mimic other animals.

Nicole smiled sweetly. "I'm sure I don't know what you mean . . . genius."

Without warning, Ana lunged for Nicole, but I caught her arms and pulled her back before she could tackle her.

"Let me go!" Ana cried, struggling against me. "She knows

where my aunt and uncle are. Don't you? *Don't you?*" she screamed, glaring at Nicole.

"Maybe," Nicole said with a shrug, seeming unfazed by Ana's outburst. She examined the nails on her right hand as if her cuticles were way more interesting than this conversation. "Maybe not."

"Where are they? What's Anubis planning to do to them?"

Nicole only tsked and said, "I hate spoilers. Takes all the fun out of it, am I right? You'll just have to wait and see." She punctuated each of the last three words by tapping Ana's nose with her index finger.

This time when Ana lunged forward, she almost managed to shake me free, and I had to grip hard around her arm. But just then Lin slid between her and Nicole. I could see Nicole's confidence falter. Before it had come out that Lin's parents had lost all their money, Lin had been one of the only girls in school who was even more of a queen bee than Nicole. And it seemed that Lin still made Nicole nervous.

"It's no use trying to get information out of her," Lin said, talking to Ana but smirking in Nicole's direction. "She's just a low-level, brownnosing lackey who probably doesn't know anything anyway."

Nicole clamped her lips shut, her grin disappearing instantly. Once again Lin had hit her target. I bet she would be crazy good at Battleship.

"Let's just go home and get some rest," Lin continued.

"Everything will look better in the morning. Except Nicole's split ends."

Nicole gasped and pawed at her blond locks. I shook my head. It was amazing. Even a shape-shifting demon with a god for a boss could still be reduced to rubble by a well-timed insult to her hair.

As for everything else looking better in the morning, I wasn't sure if that was true, but it seemed to be exactly what Ana needed to hear. She stopped fighting us, and her arms went slack. "All right," she said. "Let's go home."

Together we moved past Nicole and headed up the path. When we were several feet away, Nicole called, "Sweet dreams, ladies." She let out a high-pitched giggle, and when I whipped around, fully prepared to say something snide about her shoes, I saw her eyes flash yellow—like the hyena she was.

chapter 4

Shani

AFTER WE GOT BACK TO THE DORM THAT NIGHT, WE CLEANED and bandaged our wounds. Our heavy cat pelts had protected us from the worst of the eagle attacks. Most of our injuries were easy to treat and could be covered up with a scarf or by wearing the long-sleeved shirt of our uniform.

Doli's wounds required more attention, though. The gash in her side was deep, and the skin around it looked red and angry. The bleeding had slowed, but it still hadn't stopped completely. Thankfully, she knew exactly what to do—or her parents did. "Don't laugh," she instructed us once we'd all gathered in our room, "but this will work." She reached under her bed, wincing all the while, and pulled out a small box that her parents had made her bring with her from the reservation. It consisted of a burlap bag filled with different herbs and bits of plants. Doli pulled out a jar with a picture on the lid of a flat green leaf with what looked like spikes all around its edge.

"It's an ointment made from a mescal plant," she explained. "Sometimes it's used to stop nosebleeds, but it also helps to heal wounds. Ana, I know these two are a little squeamish"—she nodded her head at Lin and me—"so I'm going to need your help."

Under her direction, Ana cleaned Doli's wound with water, then slathered on the ointment while Doli whispered words in Navajo that she said a medicine man would usually say.

"You don't think that hocus-pocus stuff is actually going to work, do you?" Lin said.

Doli cut a glance at her as she lay down on the bed. "It isn't hocus pocus. My family believes in a combination of Western and traditional healing. Besides, I just fought a roomful of Chaos Spirit eagles, some of which came out of my T-shirt, while I was in the form of a puma, and you're going to ask me if I believe in magic?"

Lin pursed her lips. "Good point," she said. "Carry on."

It was a good point, but I still had my doubts about the treatment—until I saw Doli's bleeding stop altogether.

Later, after Ana and Lin went back to their room, Doli lay on her back with a clean bandage pressed over her wound, while I examined my own battle scars in the mirror above my dresser. Even after I'd washed the blood away and disinfected it, my ear still looked pretty nasty. That maniac ghost eagle had left a very real slice right through the top of my ear. "So much for hiding the evidence of the big fight," I said, gently touching the edge of my ear with the tip of my finger.

Doli winced. "That does look awful. Are you sure you don't want to go to the hospital for stitches?"

I shook my head. "If anybody's going to the hospital, it should be you. You're looking a little like Swiss cheese with that hole in your side."

Doli smirked. "Cute. But no, I'll be all right. I plan to tell Coach Connolly I'm not feeling well to get out of track practice for the week. By then I'll be fine. What are you going to do, though? You can't exactly wear earmuffs in the desert. People are going to ask you why half your ear is missing, and you can't say an eagle did it."

I thought for a moment, cataloging in my head all the ways one might slice open one's ear, until I hit on one that might work. "I know," I told Doli. "I'll tell people I nicked my ear while giving myself a haircut."

"Haircut? But you haven't—" Doli stopped talking when I opened my desk drawer and pulled out a pair of scissors. "Oh no . . . ," she said.

I grinned from ear to damaged ear. "Oh yes."

"Everyone's staring at your hair," Ana whispered as she sat down beside me in morning assembly the next day.

"They'll get over it," I said. "Sheesh, you'd think I had shaved it all off or something. It's just a little trim."

Actually, it was a lot more than a trim.

Truth be told, I'd ended up hacking off a little more than

I'd intended to. I still had the patch of blue hanging over my left eye, but now the rest of my hair fell in choppy waves just above my ears, showing off all the earrings and the battle wounds on my right lobe.

Doli would never trim her waist-length shiny black hair, something she said was a point of pride among her people. I kept catching her staring into our dorm trashcan, shaking her head mournfully at the severed locks. But I liked the new style; it looked punk rock to me, like I should be fronting a band that performed in underground clubs, or leading a revolution.

Of course, Temple Academy was no underground club. So it was no surprise to me that I was the center of attention.

"She looks like a lawn mower attacked her head in her sleep," I heard Lana Kapule whisper loudly somewhere behind me. Then there'd been Tanya Wallace, who had tried to look casual as she'd crossed in front of me on my way into the auditorium. She'd been pretending to text someone, but I'd heard the telltale snap of her phone's camera. She'd barely hidden her giggle as she strode away. That picture of my cut was probably already making the rounds on Instagram.

Fine, I thought. *Laugh it up, you nitwits.* If everyone focused on my hair, maybe they wouldn't notice that Doli could barely stand up straight without groaning, or that Lin had an eternity scarf looped high around her neck even though it was about a thousand degrees outside. Or that

Ana's eyes were red and puffy from crying. I considered it taking one for the team.

"Oh, who cares about your stupid hair?" Lin grumbled on the other side of me. "If anyone finds out what happened in the gym, we'll be rocking handcuffs and orange jumpsuits. That'll attract even more attention, and I'll tell you right now, orange is *not* my color."

Principal Ferris took her place behind the podium and cleared her throat, halting our conversation. Her hair was styled in her usual chic French twist, but the shirt she wore was wrinkled, and her lipstick had faded, as if she'd been biting her lip. "Good morning," she said. "I hate to start out with bad news again, but it seems I must. Last night our gymnasium was vandalized." She paused dramatically, waiting for the gasps to die down. "The damage is extensive. We don't know yet whether this is related to the vandalism of the temple. Anyway, as a result the following gym classes and sporting events will have to be postponed. . . ."

Angry murmurs from players on the sports teams raised an echoing din in the hall. "No way . . ."

"Who was it?"

"It's our money that paid for that gym . . ."

"How are we supposed to get ready for the championships now?"

Jocks . . .

It took a moment for Principal Ferris to regain control,

holding up her palms. As she began to drone on about the classes that would be postponed or canceled altogether, I tuned out, pulled my phone from my pocket, and checked my e-mail. Right at the top of the list was a message from Ms. Benitez, addressed to all four of us.

> I've arrived safely in Cancún. Meeting with some contacts this morning who may be able to help. Keep the faith. I'll be in touch when I can.

At least we still had Ms. Benitez on our side. With any luck she'd have good news for us soon. I wasn't sure how much more bad news Ana could take.

I scrolled down to the next message. It was from my mom. *Oh good,* I thought sarcastically, *time for the annual check-in.* I opened the message and skipped over all the usual nagging about keeping my grades up so I could get into a good college and not bring shame on the family. But then my eyes landed on a line that almost made me laugh out loud.

> Your sister Rana was accepted into Yale University. Since she will be in the United States, she will be able to keep a much closer eye on you.

I scoffed. Did Mom even realize that Yale was in Connecticut, all the way on the other side of the country?

How was Rana supposed to "keep an eye" on me from there? Mom had just as good a view of me from our home in Egypt. And why was my mother pretending to be so concerned about me all of a sudden? Since I'd started going to boarding schools, back when I was eight or nine years old, she had come to see me only once a year—twice if her appearance was requested by the headmistress or principal. She didn't care about having family close to me; she just wanted me to know that Rana was going to Yale, just like Solaj was at Harvard, to remind me that I should stop embarrassing them and make something of myself.

Would she think better of me if she knew that I had saved my friends' lives last night? Would she be impressed if I told her that I had the ability to turn into a lion and was using my power to try to save the world? *Probably not,* I thought. *Saving the world doesn't come with an Ivy League diploma.*

I felt a sharp elbow dig into my side. "Ow!"

"Somebody had to bring you back from La La Land," Lin whispered. "The assembly is over. What class do you have now?"

For a second I drew a blank. I guessed the e-mail from my mother had thrown me off more than I wanted to admit. "I've got Spanish. Only, Mr. Wallace is subbing for Ms. Benitez while she's away, so basically I've got Uno next period."

It had been super-easy to convince Mr. Wallace that the card game was a legit part of our curriculum, as long as we said the numbers in Spanish.

"Well, whatever class you've got, we'd better go. First period starts in a few minutes."

"And you need me to hold your hand?"

Lin rolled her eyes. "Nooo. But I'm still trying to rebuild my reputation around here—convince people that I'm not some friendless loser. It looks cooler if you aren't seen walking to class alone."

"Don't look at me," Doli said when I shot her a pleading look. "I'm going in the opposite direction."

"Me too," said Ana, shrugging one shoulder.

"See, Shani?" Lin whined. "You're all I've got."

I sighed. "Hey, Lin. Remember back when you were super-mean and wouldn't be caught dead hanging with any of us?"

Lin scrunched her mouth to the side. "Yeah."

"I kind of miss those days."

Lin gave me a begrudging smile and said, "Would you come on already? I have to walk with somebody. Might as well be you."

"I'm afraid Ms. Massri won't be attending her first-period class," said a woman's voice from behind Lin. Principal Ferris! How long had she been standing there? Lin stepped aside and looked from me to the principal and back to me again, as if she were trying to make sense of the tension in the air.

Principal Ferris turned an uncharacteristically steely gaze on me and said, "I need to see you in my office. *Now.*"

"But she has Spanish class right now," Ana said helpfully.

"I'm sure the Uno game will keep," Principal Ferris replied in a frosty tone. "Gather your things. I'll be waiting for you." With that, she stalked off toward her office.

I looked at my friends in shock.

"Does she know?" Ana asked. "A-about the gym? I mean, that we—"

"Shh!" Doli said. "Can we not talk about that so loudly?"

"I second that," Lin said. "And unless she got a forensics team down here, there's no way she could know we were there."

I shrugged. "So maybe she found out that I hacked into the airline system?"

Doli closed her eyes and sucked in a breath through her teeth. "I told you that was a bad idea."

"Oh no," Ana said, looking miserable. "If it is because of that, it's all my fault. I'll go with you and tell her so." She slung her backpack over her shoulder with a wince and started walking after Ferris. But I grabbed on to her bag and pulled her back toward us.

"Hold it right there, Cetzal," I said. "Thanks for the show of solidarity, sister, but I can handle this myself. Besides, nothing I've done is your fault."

Ana removed the jaguar necklace she always wore around her neck and held it out to me. "Want to borrow this? For protection."

I smiled at her. "Thanks," I said, "but I've already got my own." I held up my wrist to show her the gold bracelet with the lion engraved on top that I had gotten from my grandmother. "And if that doesn't work, I'll just turn into a lion and scare her to death before she can kick me out."

All three girls paled.

"Relax! I'm kidding . . . mostly."

Looking slightly relieved, Doli said, "Well, you'd better not keep her waiting." She uttered a phrase in her native language.

I gave her a blank look. "Does that mean 'good luck'?"

She shrugged. "Close enough. There's no direct translation in Navajo, so I just wished you good health."

"*Buena suerte,*" Ana added.

Lin chimed in with "*Zhù nǐ hǎo yùnqi,*" which was either "good luck" or "good riddance" in Mandarin. She claimed she wasn't sure.

"Thanks, guys," I said. I turned and walked to Principal Ferris's office, hoping my luck held out just a little bit longer.

As soon as I sat down in the chair facing Principal Ferris's desk, she narrowed her eyes at me and said, "Is there anything you'd like to tell me, Shani?"

I looked left and right, as if the answer might be written on the wall somewhere. "I . . . don't think so?"

"Really?" She leaned forward, her jaw tightening. "Nothing? Nothing at all?"

No, not nothing, I thought. There were a million things I could confess to. But if she didn't already know about the airline hack, or the gym, I certainly wasn't about to volunteer the information. Any good card player would tell you not to show your hand too early. I had to say something, though. "Uh . . . well, your French twist is looking particularly . . . French today."

Ferris shook her head and sneered at me. "How unfortunate," she said. "I thought maybe if I gave you a chance, you would confess and I wouldn't have to do this. But you leave me no other option." She pulled a remote control out of her desk and aimed it at the TV console mounted on her wall next to the bookshelf. "I'd like to show you something."

She pressed a button, and a video feed came on the screen. There I was, typing a code into the tablet in the gym and turning on the sprinklers. I gasped, and my stomach dropped into my shoes. There were *cameras* in the gym? How could I not have known that?

"As you can see, you've been caught red-handed," Ferris said, shaking her head in disbelief. "Not only did you turn on the sprinklers, which have ruined the gymnasium floor, but there's the little matter of how you were able to get into the system in the first place. Perhaps you didn't realize that those tablets keep a log of who has signed into them and when. Funny. It looks like you on the recording, but the log says *I'm* the one who signed in. Care to comment?"

Was it suddenly warm in there, or was it just me? I rubbed my grandmother's bracelet, willing it to work its protective magic. "I—I can explain," I stammered. "I did hack into the database to get your password, and I used it to turn on the sprinklers—"

"I thought as much," she interrupted. "I'm so very disappointed in you, Shani."

"B-but wait!" I cried, shooting out of my chair. "Did you even *see* what happened in the gym? If you did, then you know I had no choice. . . ."

"Conveniently enough," Principal Ferris said, rising from her chair, "the cameras in the main part of the gym were disabled." She raised one eyebrow and gave me a knowing look.

Oh my God, I thought. *She thinks* I *did it.* "Principal Ferris," I said slowly. "You have to believe me. I didn't disable any cameras in the gym. I didn't even know there *were* cameras there."

Ferris shrugged. "Be that as it may, the level of vandalism to the gym went far beyond water damage from the sprinklers, and as you can see, it seems you were the only one there."

I realized then that the other girls had never gone near the front entrance of the gym. They'd entered and exited through the side door, which is why they were never caught on camera. But I was sure some of the eagles had gone out that way. Had none of them made it onto the recording? Or were they sort of like TV vampires who couldn't be seen on film or in mirrors? An even more horrifying thought—were Doli, Lin, Ana, and I the only ones who could see the Chaos Spirits at all? I knew Jason had seen the bat back in the temple, so why couldn't Principal Ferris see the eagles?

"I swear," I tried. "I have a perfectly good reason for being there last night, and it wasn't to vandalize the gym. If you'll just listen—"

But she held up her hand to quiet me. "I know all about your reason," she said.

I stared at her in astonishment and relief. "You do?"

"Of course. I make it my business to know what's going on with my students. I know that you tried out for the tennis team recently. I know that shortly thereafter Coach Lawson started complaining about some odd things happening to her electronics—her phone dying, her Internet being disconnected, her access to certain mobile apps being blocked. . . . You wouldn't know anything about that, would you?"

I opened my mouth to speak, but nothing came out. I just went on holding my breath, hoping I might pass out on the floor and wake up somewhere else—I didn't care where. Because what could I say? I *had* messed with Coach Lawson's phone. When she had thought I was looking at pictures of her "adorable" niece, I'd really been uploading a virus here, installing parental blocks there. . . . Harmless stuff, I'd thought.

Finally I breathed out and said, in as calm a voice as I could manage, "I don't see what my trying out for the team or Coach Lawson's tech problems have to do with—"

"I think you do," Ferris cut me off. She waited a beat before saying, "I think you vandalized the gym—just as you vandalized Coach Lawson's phone—because you were upset about not making the team."

She sat down and leaned back in her chair, regarding me with a look that was both hurt and satisfied, like she was a detective who had solved a particularly heinous case and now had the pleasure of telling the criminal exactly how she'd caught her.

I was speechless. How could she think I would do something like that? I knew I wasn't exactly BFFs with the principal, but I'd been at Temple Academy for more than a year now—long enough for her to know I wasn't the kind of person who destroys a gym because she didn't make the tennis team. But from the look on her face, it seemed she'd already made up her mind that I was exactly that kind of person.

I couldn't really offer anything in my defense. If I were to tell her the truth—that Anubis had tricked us into going to the gym, that we'd fought off dozens of Chaos Spirits that served the Brotherhood of Chaos, and that I was part of an ancient order destined to stop them—she'd never believe me. She would think I was both a vandal and a schizophrenic.

It's hopeless, I thought. *Might as well skip to the fun part.*

"So what's my punishment going to be? Cleaning the bathrooms again? More community service? I could pick up trash on the side of the road, or maybe teach social media skills to senior citizens. You'd be surprised how many of them don't even know what Facebook is. . . ."

Principal Ferris stared sadly at me. "I'm sorry, Shani, but it's much too late for that. You know that Temple Academy has a three-strike policy. Even if you hadn't been in trouble twice before already for hacking, vandalizing the gym would count as all three strikes. You have cost the school thousands of dollars, and worse, you've abused my trust."

My mouth fell open. I could feel my legs begin to tremble.

"Shani, I regret to inform you that, effective immediately, you are no longer a student at Temple Academy. You've been expelled. I will inform your parents today, but you'll need to call them to discuss where you'll go next."

"Today?" My voice quivered. It wasn't until I tried to speak that I realized I'd started to cry. On the same day my mother sent me an e-mail practically begging me to stop being such a loser, she would get a phone call from my principal telling her that I'd been kicked out . . . *again*. "Can't you at least wait until tomorrow to call them?"

Her icy exterior melted a bit, but she shook her head. "No, I can't, because a cab will be here tomorrow at noon to take you to the airport. You have one day to collect your things—and yourself."

"What?" I felt my knees go weak, and I slumped down into the chair. *This can't be happening.*

Principal Ferris rose from her seat and sat in the one next to mine. She handed me a tissue and patted my hand. "I really am sorry, Shani. You're a bright girl, and I'd hoped that Temple Academy would be your home until graduation. However . . ."

She continued to talk, but I couldn't hear a word she said. My head was too full of the sound of blood rushing in my ears. I'd been kicked out? Again? How was I supposed to tell my mother? How was I supposed to tell my *friends*? I thought of Ana volunteering to come in here with me. I'd turned her down, but that was back when I'd thought it wouldn't be such a big deal.

The panic I felt taking over me made me look at Principal Ferris and ask, "What if there were others?"

She backed away from me a little, tilting her head as if she were trying to hear me better. "Others?"

"Yes," I said, more confidently. "What if I told you that I didn't do this alone?"

Principal Ferris raised her eyebrows. "Well, I hope you would tell me if there were someone else involved. It wouldn't absolve you of guilt, but it would restore a measure of trust between us. And if anyone else bore some of the responsibility, then they should share in the blame."

"Right, okay," I said, "but would it keep me from getting kicked out?"

She sighed. "Oh, that I can't promise, Shani. The fact that you were involved at all, combined with your previous record . . . It's just, Temple has rules, as you know, and I have a board of trustees to report to. The decision would not be

entirely up to me. So if you do reveal your accomplices—
provided there were any—you'd have to do it quickly, knowing full well that it might not change anything for you. But
telling me would still be the right thing to do."

"Uh . . . I need to sleep on it," I said, feeling completely
numb.

She nodded.

I walked out of her office in a daze. I'd have to break the
news to my mom eventually and thought sooner was better,
so I sat down on the bench just outside Ferris's office and took
out my smartphone. It would be about six o'clock at night in
Cairo by then, so I knew she'd be home. She picked up after
the second ring.

"Hello?"

"Hi, Mom," I said, my hand shaking so hard, I almost
dropped the phone.

"Ah, Shani! You must have gotten my e-mail. Did you want
to congratulate your sister?"

"No. I mean, yes. But first I have to tell you something—
something bad." My voice was now shaking just as hard as my
hands.

"What's wrong?" Mom said.

All I wanted was for her to tell me everything would be
okay and that I could still fix this. "I—I've been expelled, Mom.
I feel terrible. I don't know what to do."

The worst part of telling my mother bad news was always

the few seconds that passed before she reacted to it. The anticipation was almost worse than the yelling that would follow.

"*Unbelievable!* What did you do this time, Shani?"

"Nothing!" I yelled back. "At least not what they think I did."

"Nothing, huh? So they're just kicking you out because you're completely innocent?"

"No, it's just— I can't explain it all, but I swear it wasn't my fault. I was trying to help. I *did* help. Principal Ferris is going to call you later, but I want you to know that I'm innocent . . . mostly. She thinks I did something to the gym, and I was there, but she doesn't know the whole story."

Mom puffed out hard, something she did when she was truly fed up. "Well, you'd better tell her the whole story, then, the complete truth, because I'm not going to try to fix this for you, Shani. I try my best to help you. I try and I try. But I don't know what to do with you anymore."

"What are you saying, Mom?"

"I'm saying"—she took a breath—"this time you're on your own."

chapter 5
Ana

WHEN I GOT OUT OF HISTORY CLASS THAT MORNING, I found Lin waiting for me outside the door.

"Nine one one!" she said. "Emergency meeting back at the dorm. Right now!"

She grabbed my hand and pulled me along toward Radcliff Hall, pushing past other girls without sparing a single "Excuse me."

"What's going on?" I asked, doing my best to keep up.

Lin hesitated, stopping for just a moment and looking back at me. She winced. "It might be better if you hear it from Shani."

But when we got back to the dorm, it seemed Shani was in no condition to speak. She sat on her bed with her knees drawn into her chest, rocking back and forth, her mouth clamped shut. I'd never seen her like this before. It reminded me of the way I'd reacted the night I had almost hit Nicole—before I knew what she was.

"How long has she been like this?" I asked Doli.

"Ever since she came from Ferris's office," she replied.

I laid my backpack on the floor and slid onto the bed next to Shani, putting my arm around her shoulders. "So, I take it things didn't go well with Ferris."

Shani rested her forehead on her arm. "That's an understatement," she said. "Major understatement."

"All right. Well, tell me what happened. Maybe I can help."

She looked up at me, and I saw that her eyes were swimming with tears and her nose was all puffy and red. "Unless you can turn back time and stop me from getting caught on video hacking into the gym security system, you can't help me."

"*What?* They caught you on video?" I looked from Doli to Lin to see if maybe I'd just heard her wrong, but they were both nodding.

"Yep," she said, tears trailing down her cheeks. "I'm the star of my very own hidden-camera show. And now Ferris thinks I destroyed the gym because I was mad about not making it onto the tennis team."

"But that's crazy!" I cried. "You would never do something like that."

"*I* know that," Shani said, "and *you* know that. But as far as the video knows, I was the only one there that night, and you can see me on tape using Ferris's password to get into the system. Pretty open-and-shut case. Anyway, that's why she kicked me out."

I leaped out of the bed as if it were suddenly full of stinging wasps. "Kicked you out? Of *Temple*? Are you kidding me?"

Shani slumped over on the bed, grasping a pillow to her chest. "Yes, I'm kidding. Pretty funny, right? Ha-haaaaa! I'm thinking of taking my act on the road. Principal Ferris thinks I should too, apparently."

I started to pace the small dorm room. "There has to be something we can do. Let's go to Principal Ferris and tell her that we were all there, that we did it together."

"Yes," Doli said, jumping up. "Let's do it. Wildcats stick together."

But Shani just shook her head. "That's sweet, you guys, but it won't help. Principal Ferris told me that even if I were to name my 'accomplices,' it wouldn't necessarily mean that I'd get to stay. In fact, all it would do is get all of you kicked out with me."

"Maybe not," Lin said. "Not if we turn ourselves in. Besides, we're first-time offenders, not lifers like Shani." When we all shot her a look, she added, "No offense, Shani. I'm just saying—you have a record and we don't. So maybe she'd take it easy on us."

"What about your parents disowning you?" Shani asked.

Lin shook her head, then shrugged. "We both know there's a lot less for my parents to disown me from, after that accountant stole half their money. I'll take my chances."

"The point is," I cut in, "we won't let you stand alone."

"Yeah, you will," Shani said. "You have to. It's not worth the risk. Besides, we may have stopped Anubis from moving our school, but his temple is still right here below our campus. If he decides to come back, someone's got to be here to defend the school."

I growled in frustration. "Fine. But no matter where you are, we're still Hunters, and Temple Academy will still be Hunters Headquarters."

"What do you mean 'headquarters'?" Lin asked.

"As long as there are still Chaos Spirits out there, we've got to stay on the case," Doli said. "And that means having a place we agree to come back to, no matter what." She held out her hand, holding it flat. Lin slapped her hand on top of Doli's, and I put my hand on top of Lin's. We all looked at Shani expectantly. She sighed and for a moment she looked lost—like she'd once been a part of something and was now looking at it from the outside. Finally she put her hand on top of the pile, and in that moment I silently pledged that I would never stop trying to clear Shani's name and get her back into Temple, where she belonged.

Just then my phone trilled—the sound letting me know I'd

just received a text message. I moved away from the girls and dug into my backpack for my phone. The text was from Jason.

Hey, Ana. Have you seen the new pirate movie? It's rated arrrrr . . .

Despite the heaviness of the moment with Shani, I couldn't help laughing at the dumb joke and feeling my heart beat faster; that happened any time Jason texted me. As I stared down at his name in my phone, an idea occurred to me. If it worked, Shani wouldn't be going anywhere. "Let's not be so quick to say good-bye," I said, typing quickly. "I have an idea."

That night, after dinner, I stood on the track waiting for Jason. Finally I saw him jogging toward me, a sweet smile on his face. "Hey," he said, "how are you? And also, how are you?"

I smiled sheepishly. "Dork."

He laughed and gave me a quick hug. "I didn't empty-handed . . ."

"You didn't have to bring me a present," I replied, stunned that he would even think he had to. "Or, oh no, is that something friends are supposed to do? Bring each other gifts every time they hang out? If so"—I dug into my jeans pocket and pulled out an old gum wrapper and fifteen cents in change—"today is your lucky day."

"A gum wrapper *and* money?" he cried, as if I'd handed him the keys to a new car. "You're too good to me."

I shrugged. "Nothing but the best for you."

He laughed. "Well, my present is going to be kind of a letdown now. It's nowhere near as extravagant as yours." He reached into his own pocket and pulled out a Snapple bottle lid.

I took it from him and read the words printed inside: *Real Fact #349: Most cats don't like lemonade.* I smiled curiously at Jason. "Is that true?"

Jason gave me a half smile. "You could probably answer that better than I can," he said. "Anyway, I started collecting all the ones about cats, ever since I found out, you know, what you can do."

"That is so sweet," I gushed. "Thank you. I'll treasure this always." I said it as a joke, but I also meant it.

"Thank you for wanting to meet me," he said, turning serious. "It was a good excuse to get out of my house for a while. I needed a break from my mom."

Just the person I wanted to talk about. "How is she doing?"

"Not too good," he said. "Honestly? I'm worried about her."

"Really? Why?"

Jason fell silent for a moment and walked over to the risers on the side of the track. He sat down and looked up with concern in his eyes. "I know Dr. Logan wasn't who he said he was, and I'm glad he's gone, but ever since he left, Mom's been, I don't know, different."

"Different how?" I asked, sitting next to him, so close that our shoulders touched.

"She's usually so happy. But she's been really down lately. When she doesn't have to be at work, she stays in her pajamas all day long. Dr. Logan wasn't even her boyfriend. The whole thing just makes me wonder if maybe he had some kind of mind control over her, you know? That's possible, right? I mean, he was seriously evil, and he did have powers. . . ."

Suddenly I thought back to how Principal Ferris had acted like a giddy schoolgirl around Dr. Logan, and how easily she had accepted his idea to move Temple Academy. Maybe it *had* been more than simple infatuation. If he had gotten his evil claws into her mind, that would explain a lot.

"I'm not sure," I admitted. "With Anubis, anything is possible. But you know how as soon as he left, the weather cleared up?"

Jason nodded hopefully.

"Well, now that he's gone, maybe the same thing will happen for your mom. It's just going to take some time, that's all."

Jason squeezed my hand and said, "I hope you're right."

I just sat there for a while and enjoyed the thrill of having Jason hold my hand as we listened to the breeze blowing through the desert. But I had called him out there for a reason. "There's something else you should know," I said. "Something happened last night."

As quickly as I could, I told him about the whole scene in

the gym—how I'd gotten the false phone call, and how we'd been attacked by countless eagles.

"Are you serious?" Jason cried. "You got attacked by freaking *eagles* and you let me go on and on about my mom? Are you okay?" He scanned me from head to toe, as if he expected to see a gaping wound he'd failed to notice before.

"I'm fine," I said. "So are the others. We have a first aid kit at the dorm, so we patched ourselves up."

"But, Ana, you guys could've been killed. Why didn't you call me?"

"Because it all happened so fast," I said. "And we're getting pretty used to taking care of ourselves." I stopped myself from saying what was on the tip of my tongue: *What would you have done, anyway?* I shook my head, trying to clear the unkind thought away. Jason may not have had supernatural powers, but he had helped us in the temple.

"So that's what happened to the gym." He let out a low whistle. "That place was wrecked. Must have been some battle. I'm glad all of you are all right," Jason said.

"Almost all of us." I told him about Shani's meeting with his mother. "She thinks Shani vandalized the gym to get revenge on Coach Lawson. Jason, she kicked Shani out of Temple."

Jason gasped. "Whoa, that's pretty hard-core. Shani must be going crazy."

"Yeah, she is," I said, waiting for him to make the connection on his own. But when he remained silent, I had to wade in further. "There is something you can do to help, though. . . ." I shot him a pleading look, hoping he would offer what I needed without me having to ask. No such luck.

Jason brightened. "Name it."

I just stared at him, my frustration growing. Wasn't it obvious? "Maybe if somebody talked to your mom," I said finally. "I don't think she'd listen to me, but . . ."

Jason's face turned cold, and he shifted his body so he was facing me and our shoulders were nowhere near each other. "But what?" he said.

"But maybe if *you* told her how great Shani is . . ."

He stood up abruptly and strode out onto the track. "So, like . . . is that the only reason you've been hanging out with me?" He turned around suddenly, his face crumbling. "So you could get me to make my mom do stuff for you?"

"What? No!" I cried, leaping to my feet. "Of course not. I just thought maybe she would listen to you and reconsider."

"Ana, I can't get involved. My mom's job is her *job*. I'm just another student here." He shoved his hands into his pockets and kicked a stray rock onto the track. "Do you have any idea how weird it is for me sometimes? Every girl here knows I'm the principal's son. I try to tell them that I don't have any say over my mom's school decisions, but that doesn't stop them from asking me to pull all kinds of strings for them. Later curfew privileges, grade changes, access to the jet to go on shopping sprees in Europe—you name it. I'm used to not knowing if a girl is talking to me because she wants to be my friend or because she wants to get to my mom through me. But I never thought I'd have to worry about that with you."

The accusation stung. I couldn't believe he was lumping me in with all those other girls who obviously didn't care about him the way I did. "But I'm not asking for anything silly," I pleaded. "We're talking about *Shani*. She's getting kicked out for something she didn't even do."

Jason looked up at the stars, down at the gravel beneath his feet—everywhere but at me. "I know it isn't fair to Shani," he said, "but that doesn't make it okay for you to use me."

Now hurt—worse than any eagle could inflict—began to bubble up inside me. "I'm not a user, Jason. That's not me. I wouldn't ask at all if it weren't important. Can't you just ask your mom this one time . . . for me?"

Jason shook his head, and his eyes grew dark. Though he'd looked angry before, now he just seemed disappointed in a way that I would never be able to make right. He let out a hollow laugh. "I'm such an idiot," he said in almost a whisper. "All this time, I thought you liked me."

I watched helplessly as he strode away from me, toward his house. I kept my eyes on him as his figure grew smaller and smaller in the distance, eventually blurring because of the tears in my eyes.

I was a total failure. Jason would probably never speak to me again—and come noon tomorrow, Shani would be gone.

chapter 6

Shani

I DIDN'T REALLY BELIEVE I WAS GOING, UNTIL I SAW THE cab pull up outside the student center at noon sharp, just as Principal Ferris had promised.

I got to my feet. "I think my ride is here."

Principal Ferris had given my friends permission to miss classes so they could spend the morning helping me pack. I'd pretended the whole time that we were just heading for a fun vacation somewhere. But now there was no denying that I was the only one going anywhere—and I wouldn't be coming back.

"I'm going to miss you so much, roomie," Doli said, spreading her arms for a hug.

"Right back atcha, boss lady." I wrapped my arms around her, and Ana and Lin piled on until the four of us were one big lump of arms. When we pulled away, I saw that Ana was crying.

"This feels so *wrong*!" she said, rubbing at her eyes.

"No argument here," I agreed, struggling not to cry myself. I didn't want to make them feel any worse, but it was hard to hide how gutted I was. "This bites," I admitted, "but really, there was no other way it could have gone."

"What are we supposed to do now?" Lin adjusted the bun on her head.

"Hey, we still have technology. I promise, I'll totally e-mail you guys twice a day—and I'll text if I can. I'm still not sure what kind of service I'll have in Mumbai, but I'll figure it out."

"And we'll keep you updated on whatever happens with the Brotherhood of Chaos and the temple," said Doli.

"You'd better. I may not go here anymore, but I'm still a Hunter, and we're still a team. Besides, Ferris told me this morning that if I keep my grades up and my nose clean, she might let me come back next year."

"Really?" Ana said, a trail of tears drying on her face. "That's great. I wonder what changed her mind. . . ." She trailed off with a faraway look in her eyes.

"I don't know," I said, "but at least this means there's hope."

I wasn't sure I believed that, though. Not really. I had tried so hard this year—I'd gone to all my classes and done well on my tests. I'd even done my homework! And for what? I'd ended up getting kicked out anyway. *Even when I'm not looking for it,* I thought, *trouble just seems to find me.* It was like a curse I couldn't break.

Together we rolled my bags out to the cab. The driver

piled the luggage into the trunk while my friends hugged me again, and this time we all cried—even Lin. What was happening to me? I didn't do mushy. Before I knew it, the car had pulled away, leaving Temple Academy behind. As I stared out the window at the desert sands blowing in the breeze and the sun rising high over the mountains, I felt completely lost.

Now what?

Outside the Mumbai airport, it was as crowded as the New Mexico desert had been empty. As I wheeled my luggage toward the passenger pickup area, pushing through the crowd, I tried my best not to pass out. It had always been hot at Temple Academy, but this was a whole new level of heat. Already my shirt was soaked with sweat, and my head throbbed as people shouted all around me and car horns blared. How was I supposed to find my father in this mess?

I wandered aimlessly for a while, taking in all the new sights and smells—jasmine, curry, coffee—wondering if this strange place would ever feel like home. Finally I spotted a man in a white cotton shirt and matching pants holding a sign with my name on it. I headed straight for him and gave him a dead-eyed stare as I shoved my luggage toward his free hand. "He couldn't be bothered to come get me himself, huh?"

Looking unfazed, the man rolled my suitcase toward the curb. "Your father sends his regrets," he called over his shoulder. "He's a very busy man with important matters to tend to, but he said to tell you that he'll be home in time for dinner."

"Whatever," I said, annoyed and a little hurt that I didn't rank as an important matter. Still, at least Dad had agreed to let me come. Mom hadn't wanted to see me at all—at least not yet. So she had sent me to my father. It was something they'd been doing since they'd divorced when I was little. Anytime one of them got tired of dealing with me, they'd ship me off to the other parent, like a long-distance game of Ping-Pong.

The driver, who told me his name was Hemant, navigated us through the streets in his small black car, weaving through the traffic, which seemed to follow no pattern at all. We passed through packed sections of town filled with brightly colored tin roofs and barefoot children, which slowly transformed into neighborhoods with wide-open streets, two-story homes, and towering apartment buildings.

Hemant dropped me off in front of a tall glass building with terraces dotting the front. He took my suitcases out of the trunk and handed them over to the doorman, who stacked them onto a rolling cart and wheeled them inside. Then he passed me an envelope and said, "The key to the apartment is inside. It's number 14H. The doorman will show you. Welcome to Mumbai."

I followed the doorman inside, taking in the gold and silver accents and marble floor. *I guess this is the kind of swanky place you get to live in when you're a big-time diplomat.* After the doorman brought my luggage into the apartment and told me to call downstairs if I needed anything, I closed the door behind him, grateful to have a minute to myself. I hadn't seen my father in a long time—not since he'd left Egypt to serve as a diplomat in Mumbai. But we e-mailed every week, and I couldn't wait to see a friendly face.

In the meantime I decided to give myself a tour of the apartment. Then maybe I'd find out if they had Wi-Fi. I walked through a formal dining room, which reminded me that I hadn't eaten anything since breakfast. My stomach growled like Lin in tiger form. I was sure my dad wouldn't mind if I raided his kitchen. I walked into the kitchen, aiming for the refrigerator, but it was already open, with someone peering inside.

I gasped. "Dad?"

An Indian girl around my age screamed and lifted her head above the stainless steel door of the refrigerator. She was wearing a maroon-and-white school uniform not too different from the one I wore at Temple. "You scared the daylights out of me," she said in English. Her accent sounded like a mixture of Indian and British. It lilted up and down, the consonants crisp and clipped. "What's your problem?"

Huh. Maybe this place wouldn't be so different from Temple after all. I seemed to have already found the Mumbai version of Lin. The old Lin, at least. "I'm sorry," I said. "I—I must have the wrong apartment. I couldn't see you behind the refrigerator, and I thought you might be my dad."

"Oooh," the girl said, closing the door and leaning against

the refrigerator. "You must be Youssef's daughter, the criminal mastermind."

I inclined my head, trying to decide if I should be offended. I figured I'd been called worse. "Guilty as charged," I said. "I'm Shani. And *you* are?"

But in true Mumbai-Lin fashion, she didn't answer. Instead she sauntered over to me with her mouth in a grim line and her arms crossed over her chest.

"Listen, Shani, there's one thing you need to get straight right away if we're going to get along. You'd better keep your criminal mitts off my stuff. Just because we're sharing a room doesn't mean we're sharing *any*thing else, understand?"

"Share—a room?" I sputtered. "Why would we do that?" Who *was* this girl? Was she the daughter of a live-in maid or something? Even if that were the case, why would we have to share a room?

Before she could answer, the lock on the front door snicked open and my father came hurrying into the apartment.

"Shani!" he cried, rushing forward to give me a hug. "I'm sorry I didn't make it here before you. I tried, but the traffic was terrible."

"You call that traffic?" I said, wrapping my arms around his shoulders. "It's more like some kind of vehicular thunder dome."

Dad, still sharp with his wavy salt-and-pepper hair and rimless eyeglasses, laughed as he pulled away. "I've missed your sense of humor. And this haircut—is it new?"

I nodded. "It was an experiment."

"A good one," he said. "It suits you!"

I smiled. "Aw, thanks, Dad. Oh, and by the way, *who is this*?" I pointed a finger at Mumbai-Lin.

Dad's face went slack, as if he'd been hoping to put off this unpleasant business just a little bit longer. "Right, yes . . . Shani, I probably should have told you this sooner. . . ."

The girl whirled on him, her chestnut hair swishing around her long, narrow face. "You mean you didn't even *tell* her yet?" She rolled her eyes. "No wonder she's acting so confused. I thought maybe she'd suffered a brain injury."

"Tell me what?" I demanded.

Dad shifted nervously. "I was going to tell you at parents' weekend next month, but . . . well . . ."

Just then a beautiful Indian woman around the same age as my mom walked in the door. She had unlikely green eyes and skin the color of wet sand. Her hair was dark with blond highlights, and she had on long dangly earrings. She stopped next to my dad and linked her arm through his. That was when I noticed the large diamond ring on her left hand.

"I got married," my father said finally. He gave me an awkward smile and glanced at his bride adoringly. "This is your new stepmother, Sonia. And you've already met your stepsister, Kiah."

Kiah shook her head and bit out a laugh. "Didn't even tell

her," she mumbled again under her breath. "Classic." Then to me she smirked and said, "Welcome to the family . . . Sis."

But it felt like I was anything but welcome.

"Look at that," my father said with forced cheerfulness, ignoring Kiah's tone. "You're bonding already. Shani, Kiah will show you to the room you'll be sharing from now on and get you all settled in. I think you're going to like it here."

Kiah gestured for me to follow her down a long hallway with rooms on either side. She finally stopped at the last door on the left. Before she turned the doorknob, she glanced at me warily and said, "Remember. Hands off my things, understand?"

"I understand," I replied. *I understand that your computer's going to catch a really bad virus as soon as you leave the apartment.*

For the first five minutes of dinner that night, we ate in total silence. If you looked up "awkward dinner" in the dictionary, you would see a picture of the four of us huddled around a fancy granite dining room table, barely touching our veggie korma and basmati rice. But I'd never been great at holding my tongue—and that problem had only gotten worse since I'd found out I had a lion living inside me who happened to have a bit of an anger-management issue.

"Can you pass the naan, dear?" Sonia asked my dad.

"Of course, my love," he said, kissing her hand before passing her the basket of warm bread, his gaze lingering on her face. Sonia leaned toward him and kissed his cheek.

Across from me, Kiah groaned. "They've been like this ever since the wedding," she said. "You'd think with all the kissing they did at the reception, they'd have gotten it out of their systems by now."

"You were there?" I asked.

"Of course. I was the maid of honor."

A spark of anger ignited in me. So Kiah had been *in* the wedding, while I hadn't even known it was happening? That was the last straw. I finally slammed my fork down onto my plate, sending bits of rice scattering across the table. "How could you not tell me you got married, Dad?" I yelled. "And don't say you never found the right time. You e-mail me every week. *Every week!* You don't think in one of those e-mails you could have skipped the part about the weather and, I don't know, told me you went and got a *whole new family*?"

Dad set his own fork down next to his plate. He'd clearly known I would blow up about this eventually. He just hadn't known when. At least he had the sense to look ashamed of himself. "I was going to tell you," he said. "But it seemed like the kind of news I should tell you in person."

"So you let me walk in here and get ambushed?"

Dad started to respond, but Sonia placed her hand over his as if to say, *Youssef, let me handle this.* "Shani, you're not being fair to your father. He really was planning to tell you when he saw you for parents' weekend, but . . ." Her eyes slid to the side, clearly not wanting to say anything distasteful that would offend me. Good thing Mumbai-Lin had no such hang-up.

"But then you ruined that by becoming a real criminal and getting expelled from your school," Kiah finished for her mother.

"Kiah!" Sonia scolded. "Manners."

Kiah let out an exasperated sigh. "Sorry, Mother. What I meant to say was, your father's plans were foiled when you experienced a lapse in judgment that resulted in your relocation to our loving home." She smiled sweetly at her mother. "Better?"

Her mother frowned at her. "That's enough."

Dad sighed. "Putting aside Kiah's rudeness for the moment"—he aimed a look of warning her way, and she wiped the smirk off her face—"she and Sonia are right. It was your actions that forced you to meet them this way. Your mother told me that you were finally doing well at Temple Academy before this incident. None of us expected that you would do anything to get expelled."

Kiah laughed out loud then. "Why not? Isn't this the eighth school to kick her out?"

Fourth, I thought miserably. But I didn't think that sounded any better than "eight."

"I said that's enough, Kiah!" Sonia said firmly.

My new stepsister held up her hands in surrender, but she was clearly amused by my suffering. Usually I had a quick comeback ready for people like her. Living with Nicole for a semester had really honed my skills. But as I looked around the table at all of their faces, I saw myself the way they must have seen me—as a troublemaker, a loser, a budding felon. Not exactly anyone's idea of an ideal family member.

I stared down at my plate, shoving the potatoes and almonds from one side of my plate to the other. This was one of my favorite dishes, and usually I would have devoured it in less than five minutes. But my appetite had shriveled up and died—sort of like any hopes I'd had for the future.

"Can I be excused?" I asked at last. "I just want to go to my room and lie down."

"You mean my room," Kiah said. "You're just visiting."

"The room belongs to both of you for now," Dad corrected with a sigh, "and no, you may not be excused. In this house we all have chores. Tonight you'll wash dishes. There are no free rides here."

I sighed, wondering if there was an app that would make everyone forget how badly I'd screwed up.

Even though the apartment had a dishwasher right next to the sink, they never used it. Sonia explained that they had the money to afford a few luxuries, but they believed that doing things for themselves kept them humble and gave them character. All it seemed to be giving me was pruny fingers.

"Can I help?" Dad asked, joining me at the sink.

"It's a free country," I said, shifting to make room for him. "Right? I keep forgetting I'm not in America anymore."

"Yes," he said. "India is a democracy. As soon as I have some time off from work, I'll show you around so you can see what a beautiful country it is." He rolled up his sleeves and picked up a dish, running it under the faucet. Then he grabbed a soapy sponge and moved his hand in a circle around the plate. I did the same, and for a few seconds we were in sync.

"I'm sorry about springing all of this on you, Shani," he said suddenly. "I am. But you have to understand. In my day, people didn't tell their families important news over e-mail or even by phone. You went around and told everyone in person out of respect. I wanted to show you the same respect."

I nodded, glad to be hearing him out for the first time without anyone else listening in. "Okay. I get that," I said. "But why didn't you come to see me sooner?"

He gave me a rueful smile. "I know you think I'm rich, Shani, but that simply isn't the case. Especially now with your sister Solaj in college, and Rana heading to Yale in the fall. Don't you know that if I could, I'd come see you every month? I would have loved for all three of my daughters to be a part of the wedding too. But I didn't want any of you to miss time from school, and flying to see you on a moment's notice just wasn't possible. That's why I was so looking forward to next month. I couldn't wait to tell you everything."

I sneaked a quick peek at my dad, noting how much younger he looked than most of my friends' fathers, even though they were the same age. He still had his diplomat ID clipped to his shirt pocket, which reminded me that he spent most of his day trying to make life better for other people. "Dad, can I ask you something?"

"Anything," he said.

I hesitated. "Well, I didn't even know you were . . . I mean, when did you start dating again?"

He glanced at me, as if trying to gauge how much he should tell me. He seemed to decide I was old enough to hear it all.

"Do you know how your mother and I met?" he asked. When I shook my head, he said, "We met through a match-maker in Cairo. The first time I saw your mother was in her living room, surrounded by her entire family. We met there twice more and decided to get married a few months later."

I nearly dropped the plate I was holding. "You mean—you barely knew Mom when you married her?"

"That's right," he said. "Our marriage was arranged, or what they sometimes call a 'salon marriage.' We were both so young, but both of our families were pressuring us to marry, so we agreed to it. For the most part, we were happy too, especially when you girls came along. But in many ways we remained strangers to each other. With that distance eventually came resentment. After we divorced, I didn't see anyone.

Not for a long time. I didn't even know how to go about dating, since I had never really done it."

"So how did you end up with Sonia?"

He smiled. "In the best way. We were friends first. When I moved to Mumbai, I decided I needed to get familiar with the city as quickly as possible. So I signed up for a tour. Sonia was my guide. We hit it off right away and started spending time together as friends. We'd both been divorced and had children, so we had that in common. We talked for hours and made each other laugh. I never knew it could be that way. Soon I realized that without even noticing, I had fallen in love."

"And she did too?" I asked.

"I hope so," he said, laughing. "Otherwise, agreeing to marry me was a big mistake."

I laughed too, then said, "In that case I'm happy for you. I just wish you had told me."

"I know, sweetheart. But like I said, I thought I was going to see you soon and my news could wait until then. There's no way I could have known that you would be expelled again."

I winced.

"I know that must be a sore subject," he continued. "Are you ready to talk about it yet? I'd love to hear your side."

I shook my head. I hadn't figured out what I was going to tell him. I didn't want to lie, but the truth would land me on a psychiatrist's couch. "Not tonight, okay?" I begged.

"All right," he said. "We'll leave it alone. For now. Are there any other questions you want to ask me?"

"Only about a million," I replied. "But let's start with what school I'll go to now. Not that I'd mind a little vacation, but I don't want to fall too far behind."

Dad picked up a kitchen towel and started drying the wet dishes and stacking them in the cupboard. "Actually," he said, "I've hired a private tutor so you can be homeschooled for the rest of the semester."

"Homeschooled?" I dropped the sponge into the soapy water and faced him. "Is that your way of punishing me?"

Dad raised his eyebrows in genuine surprise. "Punishing you? I thought you would love it. I thought you could use a break, some time to regroup . . ."

"A break, sure, but homeschooling is like being grounded *all the time*. I'd never get to leave this apartment, and the only people I'd talk to all day would be the tutor and the doorman. You really can't see how lonely I would be?"

Dad breathed out hard and rolled his sleeves back down. "The truth is," he started, "I did try to get you into Kiah's school, but they wouldn't take you. They took one look at the disciplinary actions in your file and . . ." He spread his hands in front of him as if the rest were self-explanatory. "Maybe next term will be different. Once your grades are up and you've shown that you can handle being in a school setting again, maybe they'll give you another chance. But for now this is the best I could do. I'm sorry."

I hung my head in shame, feeling my stomach churn unpleasantly. I was a total embarrassment to him. I couldn't even imagine what it must have felt like for him to beg schools to let me in, only to be told that his daughter was a reject. Of course Kiah's school hadn't wanted me. What did I expect?

"Okay," I said, feeling tears building up behind my eyes. "Thank you for trying. May I be excused now?"

"Yes," he said. "But first, how about a hug for your old dad?"

I ran into his arms and pressed my face against his chest, careful to turn my damaged ear away from him. Then I sobbed into his shirt, clinging to him for dear life. I had needed this hug ever since I'd been kicked out of Temple Academy.

"Shh, shh." He kissed the top of my head. "I know there have been a lot of surprises for you today, and I'm sorry about that, but everything's going to be okay now. Do you believe me?"

I nodded against his chest. I wanted to believe him, anyway. But for now, pretending would have to do.

After I pulled away and wiped my face, I asked the really important question, the answer to which really would make me feel at home and like maybe one day things would go back to normal.

"Dad . . . will you give me your Wi-Fi password?"

He laughed. "I can't believe it took you this long to ask." He pulled out his wallet and dug around before handing me a slip of paper. "I had a feeling you'd need one, so I set up an account just for you. Here's your username and password. Feel free to change it to whatever you'd like." For the third time that day, I hugged my father. Room and board were great, but nothing says you care like giving a girl her own Wi-Fi account. Just before I left the room, I stopped in the doorway and turned back. "Dad, one more question."

"Go ahead."

"Are you happy? I mean, with Sonia?"

He smiled, his eyes no longer droopy or sad. "Very."

"All right," I said. "Then I am too."

Back in the room, I looked around at the posters and pictures Kiah had plastered all over the walls. There were some from Bollywood movies I'd never heard of, and some American ones, like the *Twilight* poster that featured Jacob and his pack of wolves. Then there were collages of Kiah and her friends mugging for the camera, and a few of Kiah in a beautiful red sari that she must have worn to the wedding. She had covered nearly every surface. The only part of the room that was clearly mine was the twin bed that had been shoved into the corner farthest from the window. Kiah had left a note on it that said, *This one's yours. Don't even THINK of sitting on mine.*

Yeah, this roommate situation was going to work out just great.

I sat on my bed and turned on my phone for the first

time since arriving. Dad must have already switched me to an international plan, because as soon as the screen loaded, I saw that I had at least ten texts and twice as many e-mails from my friends back at Temple.

> How are you? Are you okay? Sorry about all the blubbering yesterday. (Ana)
> OMG come back! Ferris wants to give me a new roommate. NO! (Doli)
> I miss you. Tell anybody, and I'll deny it. (Lin)
> Morning assembly was boring without you. (Ana)
> Your haircut started a trend. They're calling it the Shani. Saw three already today. (Doli)
> Any cute boys in India? Details, please. (Lin)

I knew I should write back and tell them about everything that had happened. But I didn't know where to start. Plus, I didn't want to start crying again. I settled for sending out a group text:

> Don't worry. Made it to Mumbai in one piece. I MISS U GUYS SOOO MUCH!!! TTYL

That would have to be enough for tonight. I pulled my pajamas out of my suitcase and changed, then put my regular clothes back in the case. No surprise, Kiah hadn't left me any room in the closet or in her dresser. I lay back on the bed and closed my eyes, hoping that Lin's words from the other night would be true for me too: *Everything will look better in the morning.*

I really hope so, I thought, and fell asleep.

chapter 7
Shani

I GROANED AND SLOWLY OPENED ONE EYE. I KNEW I SHOULD have gone to the bathroom before I fell asleep. But my internal clock was all thrown off. The clock on the nightstand next to Kiah's bed said that it was 2:17 a.m., but that meant it was 1:47 p.m. in New Mexico. Was I half a day ahead or half a day behind? All I knew was that here it was the middle of the night, and I had to go . . . bad. The last thing I wanted to do was drag myself out of bed, but I refused to add "wet the bed" to my list of accomplishments this year.

I sat up, still half-asleep. Thankfully, the bathroom was just down the hall on the right. I made it there and back to my room—excuse me, *our* room—without bumping into any walls, but before I climbed into bed, I noticed that Kiah wasn't in hers. *That's weird*, I thought. Had she been there when I'd gotten out of bed? I hadn't noticed.

I stepped toward her bed to check on her. Maybe she had fallen on the floor?

That was when something grabbed me from behind and pulled me down with a thud.

My heart leaped into my throat, and icy panic shot down my spine. "Gah!" My head bounced off the hardwood floor, and everything went black for a few moments. When I came to, my vision was blurred and my stomach heaved. I felt dizzy and confused.

"What's going—" But before I could get the whole question out, something clamped down on both my arms and started dragging me down the hall toward the living room.

"Hey!" I yelled, flailing my legs and trying to yank my arms out of the vise grip they were in, but it was no use. Whatever had me continued to jerk me along. My pajama top had crept up, and my bare back scraped along the hardwood floor, the friction burning my skin. My neck grew slick with sweat, and my heart thumped out of control. *What is happening?*

This has to be a dream, I thought frantically. *Wake up, Shani! Wake up!* But if it was a dream, it was the most vivid one I'd ever had. All the lights in the apartment were off, so I couldn't see anything; I could only focus on the pain in my shoulders and the sharp objects tearing through my pajama sleeves and scratching at my skin.

Suddenly I was dumped onto the area rug in the living

room, my arms feeling like they had been stretched into noodles. I rubbed my sore head and tried to will my eyes to adjust to the dark. I craned my head to see who—or what—had dragged me in here, but I was completely alone. In my blindness I heard the front door open with a creak. And then I caught the unmistakable whiff of feral dogs.

It was a common enough smell on the streets of Cairo, where I'd grown up. There were times when it seemed like there were more stray dogs than humans there, and some of them had been so wild, they were closer to wolves than dogs. Once that rank smell got into your nostrils, it was almost impossible to forget. That was what I smelled now—the stink of sewers and day-old meat rising up from hot breath near my face.

I should have run, but fear had frozen my limbs in place.

I lifted my head enough to make out several pairs of glowing yellow eyes circling around me, restless and primal. Before I could make myself move, the largest dog let out a terrifying growl, and they all attacked as one.

I screamed at the top of my lungs and curled into a ball, trying to protect my head. I felt their fangs rip at my pajamas. Any minute they would find just the right spot on my throat and this fight would be over. I had to turn into a lion—right *now*—but I couldn't concentrate. I had zoomed right by fear and arrived straight at abject terror.

Come on, Shani, get it together! Show these mutts who

they're messing with. I pictured my heavy lion paws, my golden fur and powerful haunches. I opened my mouth to let out a roar, but all I heard was the scream of a scared teenage girl. Why wasn't I changing? I felt sleepy and sluggish, like I'd been drugged. My body wouldn't cooperate with me. All I could do was kick out wildly with my legs and fists. One of my feet connected with a wet snout, and the dog whimpered and backed away, lowering its head so I could see the ugly scar that snaked across the top of its skull, the skin around it balding and pale.

But the others seemed even more determined to tear me apart. The more I kicked, the more they grabbed at my arms, pulling at me with their glistening teeth, biting down on my thigh, ripping through the fabric . . .

"NO!" I screamed, my throat on fire.

"Shani?" I heard my father's voice call from his bedroom, and a few seconds later a light clicked on in the hall. As if responding to a whistle only they could hear, the dogs broke off their attack and scrambled for the door.

"Dad," I croaked, struggling to sit up. I touched my arms and legs, wondering if the dogs had broken through the skin. Was I bleeding? I hugged myself, trying to get a grip on reality.

Dad appeared in the doorway. He flicked on the light. "What's going on here?" he said.

I looked up, reaching out for him. But then I noticed that he wasn't looking at me. I turned around to follow his gaze. There, sitting on the overstuffed chair at the edge of the rug, in blue silk pajamas, was Kiah. Where had she come from? Our eyes connected for a long moment, and she wiped her mouth with the back of her hand. Other than the three of us, the room was empty, and the front door was firmly locked. Nothing was out of place—not even Kiah's hair.

"That's what I want to know," Kiah said, standing up and edging around the area rug, giving me a wide berth, as if I were the dangerous animal. She turned to my father. "I was sound asleep when I heard Shani get out of bed. She was mumbling something about dogs and wasn't making much sense, so I followed her. She must have been sleepwalking."

"Sleepwalking!" I exclaimed. Was she joking? I was all set to call her a liar, but then—*was* she lying, or had I really been asleep? I felt so groggy, like my head was full of cotton. Maybe she was telling the truth.

"I tried to wake her up," Kiah went on, "but whenever I went near her, she screamed. So I just sat here and watched over her to make sure she didn't throw herself out a window or anything. She thrashed around a lot and yelled, and that's when you came in."

Dad slid his eyes over to me as if to confirm the story, but for the life of me, I couldn't figure out what was real. I *had* hit my head pretty hard. My eyes still felt so heavy, and the more I thought about a pack of wild dogs breaking into the apartment to attack me, the less likely it seemed. I thought back to Principal Ferris telling me they hadn't seen anything on the tape besides me. She hadn't seen any eagles. Maybe I was crazy and had imagined the whole thing. Maybe all the Wildcats were. Which meant this could all be in my mind too.

"I don't know what to say, Dad," I said. "I can't think straight. And I have a headache." I massaged the knot that was swelling on the back of my head. Could I seriously have thrown *myself* onto the floor?

Dad knelt beside me and put his hands on my shoulders. "Sounds like a bad case of jet lag," he said. "Traveling as far as you have has been known to cause all sorts of side effects— some of them pretty serious. Sleepwalking, migraines. I'll see about getting you checked out by a doctor in the morning. But for now let's all try to get some sleep."

He helped me to my feet and walked me all the way to the bedroom, kissed me on my forehead, and said good night. I climbed into my bed feeling like I'd been beaten up, my heart still hammering away in my chest. I did my best to slow my breathing, to think happy thoughts so I could go back to sleep. But something was still bothering me.

"Kiah, did you see how I hit my head on the floor?" I asked, but her only response was a deep steady snore. Kiah was already sound asleep.

When I woke the next morning, the room was warm and bright, the sun streaming through the sheer white curtains. Someone was snoring peacefully in the other bed, and for a brief, happy second, I thought it was Doli and we were in our dorm room in Radcliff Hall. But then I remembered. I was in Mumbai, and Doli was back at Temple. I checked the clock: 8:30 a.m. Right now Doli was probably having dinner with Lin and Ana, or watching TV in the common room, while I was stuck here with Kiah. I glanced around at the pictures of her friends, her favorite celebrities, her oh-who-cares-what on the walls that continued to shout, *My Room, My Room, My Room*. I was almost surprised that she hadn't peed all over it like a dog to mark her territory.

The rest of the house was still quiet. I crept out of bed and inspected myself in the full-length mirror mounted on the back of the door. I had scratches on both arms and a gouge on my hand that I would swear was from a dog's tooth. Could I have scratched myself? I doubted it. I barely had any nails to speak of. Not as a human, anyway.

I took my bathrobe out of my suitcase and put it on, then knelt down and swiped my hand across the hardwood floor, feeling for claw marks. There had to be some evidence that I'd been dragged out of there by an animal, but I couldn't find a single scratch in the smooth brown wood. I stood up and grabbed my phone, which I'd kept by my side all night, and slipped it into the pocket of the bathrobe, then went into the living room. Maybe if I saw it in the light of day, I thought, without anyone around to confuse me, I could think clearly about last night.

Did I dream it?

I *must* have. But even my Hunter dreams hadn't been *that* vivid. I sank down to the carpet and dragged my fingers through the plush fibers, trying to recall how I had ended up there. Kiah had said I'd walked, but I remembered being dragged across cold hardwood and then dumped onto this very soft carpet. Considering I'd never even been in this apartment before yesterday, how could I have dreamed those details so perfectly? How would I—

My hand, which had been running through the luxurious rug, suddenly came across a tiny pink scrap of cotton. I plucked it up with my fingers and held it to the light.

It was from my pajamas.

I didn't dream any of it! Without even looking, I knew that there was a matching hole somewhere on the pajamas I still had on, and I knew this material was strong enough that I couldn't have ripped it with my bare hands. I would have needed a knife—or claws.

And if dogs had really been in the apartment, that meant somebody had to have let them in.

That person had to be Kiah.

One thing was for sure. I would have to watch my back from now on. Kiah was more than just obnoxious—she was dangerous. *But why?* I wondered. Surely she wouldn't have tried to kill me just so she could have her room to herself again.

Just then I heard the clink of a spoon against a cup behind

me. I turned to find my dad standing in the adjoining kitchen, smiling. "Up nice and early, I see," he said. "I'm not surprised. You pretty much passed out right after dinner yesterday."

"Yeah, I guess I did," I agreed.

"I thought I'd make us some chai. Sound good?"

"Sure, sounds great," I said, following him to a bar stool on the other side of the kitchen island while he pulled out a silver teakettle, filled it with water, and set it to boil. "Dad, can we talk?" I asked tentatively.

"Of course," he said. "You can talk to me about anything."

"It's about last night . . ."

Dad waved me off with a flick of his hand. "No need to be embarrassed, sweetheart. It could have happened to anyone."

"Embarrassed?" I said, crinkling my eyebrows. "Why would I—"

"After all," he continued, "you have so much on your mind right now."

"Well, that's true, but—"

"Not to mention the jet lag. Plus, did you know you used to sleepwalk when you were small?" He opened another cabinet and pulled out two teacups.

"What? No, I didn't know that. But I don't think—"

"I remember this one time when you were five years old. You got up in the middle of the night, and I had to stop you from walking right out the front—"

"DAD!" I slammed my hands on the counter, and Dad

startled, clacking the teacups together. "I don't feel embarrassed, and I don't think I was sleepwalking. I think . . ." I took a deep breath. "I think Kiah was trying to hurt me. Look!" I held out my arms, turning them this way and that so he could see all the scratches cutting into the flesh in angry red lines.

Dad set the teacups down and took a step away from me, his eyes wide. "You can't be serious," he said. "Shani, you fell over while you were sleepwalking. Any number of things could have caused those scratches. Why would you blame Kiah?"

"I wouldn't say something like that to you if I didn't believe it," I said. "I think she let some dogs from outside in . . . I'm not sure exactly what happened, but—"

"But you're willing to accuse your stepsister of something so terrible?" he finished for me. He looked down at the floor and shook his head. When he lifted his eyes to me, I saw a touch of anger there, but mostly a profound disappointment. "You know, Shani, I understand that all of this is strange for you, and I considered the possibility that you and Kiah would not be instant friends, but this . . . This is ridiculous."

"But, Dad, why would I accuse her of something if I didn't think she'd done it? That is *so* not my style. I even have proof." I opened my hand to reveal the piece of pink fabric. "I found this on the carpet in the living room. It was torn off my pajamas. I didn't do that. Dad, I remember being attacked last night, and Kiah was the only one there."

"Oh, Shani," he said, and this time he looked like he felt

sorry for me. "Your mother told me that you've been troubled, but I didn't realize how serious the problem was until just now. Don't you see that Kiah is family? You don't need to feel threatened by her, and you certainly don't need to make up wild stories to get me on your side." He took the scrap of fabric from me and dumped it into the trash under the sink.

I couldn't believe this. I knew my version of events sounded far-fetched, but didn't I deserve the benefit of the doubt? Kiah might have been his stepdaughter, but I was his *blood*! I realized with a sinking feeling that I was on my own, just as Mom had said I was. She'd been right all along.

Just then my phone beeped in my pocket. I pulled it out and saw I had a text from Ana. I swear, it was like somehow she knew I needed a reminder that I had friends. I swiped my finger across the screen to read the whole message, but my father reached across the counter and snatched the phone out of my hands.

"This is part of the problem," he said, looking at the phone as if it were a pack of cigarettes. "You've always been more interested in digital life than real life, and it looks like you're starting to have trouble telling the difference. I think maybe you need time away from electronics to clear your head."

"Wait, what?" I got to my feet. "Dad, you can't do that to me."

"I'm not doing anything *to* you; I'm doing this *for* you," he said. "You can hold on to your laptop since you will need that for school, but it doesn't leave this house." He slipped my phone into his pocket and went back to getting the tea ready.

All right, stay calm, I told myself. *This isn't that bad. I get to keep my laptop, which means I can still e-mail my friends.* I backed out of the kitchen before Dad could change his mind. But I had just reached the doorway when he said, "One more thing: I'm turning off the Wi-Fi during the day, and disabling your password altogether. You won't be needing it after all."

The teakettle let out a long, loud whistle that sounded like a scream.

chapter 8

Ana

"This is like some kind of nightmare," I said. "I'm ruined."

Lin, Doli, and I were walking back to the dorm from English class. I was still clutching my paper on *Macbeth* in my hands, peeking at it every once in a while, hoping against hope that the next time I looked, the B minus written there would have magically changed into an A.

"Oh, boo hoo." Lin pulled her own paper out of her backpack. It had a large red D right at the top. "I would be thrilled with a B minus right about now, so quit being so miserable."

"It's just that English is usually my best subject. I don't know what happened!"

"Don't be so hard on yourself, Ana," Doli said. "You've had a lot of other stuff on your plate—a full load of classes, taking care of the cat, trying to prevent an ancient evil cult from returning the world to an apocalyptic state of chaos. . . . Your schoolwork was bound to suffer."

I smiled. Leave it to Doli to put everything in perspective. "I know you're right. Still, my aunt and uncle aren't going to be too pleased when they see . . ." I let the words trail off and fade away, feeling a familiar dread settle into my stomach. I gulped. I had been about to say that they wouldn't be happy when they saw my grades. *But right now I'm not even sure where they are . . . or if I'll ever see them again.* I quickly banished the terrible thought from my mind. I couldn't give up on them. I had to trust Ixchel to uncover the truth, and I had to hold on to my faith that I'd see my family soon. But still, the dread lingered. "Scratch that. What I wouldn't give to have Uncle Mec here, nagging me about my grades," I said.

Doli nodded and patted me on the back. "I know. But hey, we can do the next best thing. Let's go Skype Shani. She'll rag on your grades for you."

"Just don't ask her to hack into the system and change your grade—not even as a joke—because she'd do it," Lin added.

"Roger that," I said.

It felt strange walking into Doli and Shani's room without Shani. Almost all of her things were gone, but Doli had refused to take over Shani's space, in case she came back. So on one side of the room were pictures and books and a red throw that Doli's grandmother had made—and on the other side was an empty desk and a stripped mattress.

"Let's see how Shani's doing." Doli opened her laptop

and connected to Skype, but then she leaned back, looking puzzled. "That's weird. She's not online."

I checked the time. "Well, it *is* pretty late in Mumbai right now. Maybe she's asleep," I said.

"Maybe," Doli replied. "She hasn't been online in a long time, though. It's not like her."

"Didn't you say she hadn't seen her dad in months?" Lin asked. "Maybe she's just spending lots of time with him, catching up."

"I hope so," I said. "I'd hate to think she's avoiding us because she's mad that we didn't back her up about what happened in the gym."

Doli shook her head. "No way. It was her idea for us to keep quiet. She knows we would have had her back if it would have made any difference. No, I'm sure she'll get in touch when she can."

I sat on Shani's empty bed and sighed. "In the meantime let's call Ms. Benitez to see how things are going in Cancún. She probably would have called if she'd found my aunt and uncle, but it's worth a try. I could really use some good news."

"You've got it." Doli brought up Ms. Benitez's photo and clicked to initiate a conversation. But no one picked up. The computer just rang and rang. "Guess she isn't there right now."

I chewed on my bottom lip. "Okay, but have any of you heard from her at all since that first e-mail?"

"Not me," Lin said.

"Me either," added Doli.

"That makes it unanimous," I said. "I've e-mailed her a few times to see how the search was going, but she never answered."

The three of us exchanged worried glances.

"She's probably just out looking for your aunt and uncle," Doli reasoned.

I shook my head. "I have a bad feeling, and if being a Wildcat has taught me anything, it's to trust my instincts." I took out my phone and pulled up the name and number of the hotel in Cancún where Ms. Benitez was supposed to be. I showed it to Doli. "Let's try calling the hotel."

Doli dialed the number, and after two rings a male voice said, "*Buenos días.* The Riviera Maya Inn. How may I help you?"

"Yes," Doli jumped in, "we were just trying to reach someone who checked in a couple days ago, Yvette Benitez?"

"Certainly. Hold for one moment, please." He put us on hold for a few seconds, and when he came back on the line, he said, "I'm sorry. Ms. Benitez did have a reservation, but she never checked in."

"No, that can't be right," Doli said. "Can you check again?"

"I assure you, our records are accurate," he insisted, sounding a little annoyed.

I leaped up and leaned toward the speaker. "Sir? Could you maybe try"—I winced, knowing how crazy this would sound—"Mrs. Ixchel?"

"Excuse me?" the man said. "What was that name?"

Lin gave me a quick shake of her head and closed her eyes, as if I were embarrassing her in public. "Ixchel," I repeated. "*I-x-c-h-e-l*."

There was a pause and the sound of a keyboard clacking. "I have nothing in that name," said the man. After thanking him, we hung up.

Doli's eyes were wide. "She never got to the hotel."

"Yeah, that isn't good," Lin added. "Do you think something happened to her?"

"Maybe," Doli said. "If the Brotherhood really is setting up camp in Cancún, maybe they could sense her coming and they were waiting for her. If they were going to attack her, it would have been before she met up with her contacts. Ana, I bet that whoever is holding your aunt and uncle have Ms. Benitez now too."

"So what do we do?" Lin asked in a strained voice.

"I go after her," I answered immediately. "The only reason Ms. Benitez went to Cancún was to help me. If she ended up in danger, it's my fault. I won't leave her out there to fend for herself."

Lin lifted her perfectly tweezed eyebrows. "You, as in by yourself? Uh-uh, no. We already let Ms. Benitez and Shani go off on their own, and now they're both missing in action. The rest of us stick together from here on out. Besides, how would you get there? I'm guessing you don't have hundreds of dollars in your pocket to pay for a flight, and with your aunt and uncle missing . . . well, they aren't around to cover your travel expenses. Plus, I know that *I* travel internationally all the time, but do you two even have passports?"

"Actually, I do," I said. "I got one last summer before my family and I drove up to Canada to see Niagara Falls."

"I have one too," Doli added. "Coach Connolly had me get one in case I got to compete in the track meet in England at the end of the year."

"Okay," Lin conceded. "We've all got passports. But unless you have three flying broomsticks in your backpacks or some cash I don't know about, we're stuck."

"No, we're not," Doli said. Lin and I turned to her with curious stares. "Isn't it obvious? We'll take the Temple Academy jet."

"I thought of that," I said. "But it's only supposed to be used for emergencies."

"I'd say your aunt and uncle—and our teacher—being missing counts as an emergency," Doli replied.

I got up and paced the room. "Right, but we can't tell Principal Ferris that without telling her all the rest of it. She'll think we've lost our minds."

"So we'll come up with something else. All we need to do is convince her that we really need to borrow the jet, and we need it right away." Doli smiled confidently.

Lin laughed. "Oh, is that all?" she scoffed. "That should be a breeze."

"Trust me." Doli's eyes sparkled. "I have a plan."

A few hours later we were on our way to Principal Ferris's office. I had swapped my *Macbeth* paper for one I had just written. It was called "Mayan Culture and Its Influence on Modern-Day Hispanic Identity." Pretty serious-sounding stuff, but it was mostly full of things I'd learned from Aunt Teppy and Uncle Mec. They'd taught me so well, I'd been able to write the paper from memory.

"Remember, just stick to the story, exactly like we rehearsed it," Doli said. "Why do you need to borrow the jet, Ana?"

I repeated the story we had worked out. "We're doing a research assignment on the Mayans for Spanish class, and we need to visit the Mayan villages in person in order to make sure our facts are correct."

"Good. And, Lin, why don't we need an adult to go with us?"

"Because Ms. Benitez is already there and is going to meet us. Plus, Antonio will stay in town with the jet until we're ready to come back."

"Perfect. I think we're ready."

Together we entered the main building and turned down the hallway, feeling confident. But as we got closer, I saw something that made me stop in my tracks. Jason was sitting on the bench outside Principal Ferris's office—and he wasn't alone. Sarah Gopolan, who I recognized from my math class but had never really spoken to, sat beside him, laughing at something he'd just said. I hadn't noticed before how pretty Sarah was, and seeing her so close to Jason, seeing him laugh with her, felt like getting punched in the stomach.

"Uh-oh," said Lin. "Do you want to leave and come back later?" I had told Lin and Doli what had happened with Jason. Since our argument, he hadn't replied to any of my texts, and he'd never waited for me after morning assembly again. Whenever I saw him around campus, he pretended he suddenly had to be somewhere in the opposite direction. Were we even friends anymore? Were we anything?

"No," I replied. "This is more important than avoiding him."

When Jason looked up and saw me, his mouth fell open. "Ana . . ."

Sarah, glancing from me to Jason, suddenly looked nervous. "Um, I should really get going. I have to call my parents and let them know what your mom said about the extra credit projects." She touched his arm. "But I'll see you later, okay?"

He nodded dumbly. Sarah gave the rest of us a quick wave and hurried away.

Saving me from the awkwardness of talking to Jason, Principal Ferris suddenly ducked her head out of her office and said, "Ms. Cetzal, right on time. Please come in."

I did my best to put the image of Jason's caught-in-the-act

face behind me. I had to try to focus on what was important. We sat across from Principal Ferris, who laced her fingers together. "How can I help you today?"

"Um." I cleared my throat and straightened in my chair. "We came to ask"—*why your son was out there talking to Sarah Gopolan*—"if maybe you would"—*tell me if they're friends or more than friends*—"give us permission to"—*transfer Sarah to another school, preferably in Siberia*—"borrow the school jet."

Principal Ferris frowned. "The school jet? Why would you girls need to use the jet?"

"Because . . . ," I started. *Because Jason was the first person on this campus who was really nice to me. Because I still have the Snapple bottle cap in my pocket and a pirate joke he texted me on my phone. Because he saw me transform into a jaguar and accepted me anyway. . . .*

"Ana!" Doli said, snapping her fingers in my face. "Didn't you want to tell Principal Ferris something about the paper you wrote?" She tapped the report sitting on my lap.

I took a deep breath. "Yes, absolutely. Uh . . . I wrote this report." I slid it across the desk to her. "And we're working on a project for class, and . . ." The whole speech I had practiced all afternoon seemed to have fallen out of my head.

"You'll have to excuse Ana," Doli jumped in. "She's so excited about the research project we're working on for Spanish class, she can hardly contain herself. You see, Ana's Mayan heritage has given her a great respect for the culture and its people. Right, Ana?" Doli pulled the leather necklace she always wore out of her shirt and held the puma figurine in her hand. She shot me a pleading look, and I remembered everything. This mission was bigger than any cute boy. It was about saving Ms. Benitez and my family—and maybe the world.

I smiled. "That's right, Doli. In fact, I'm probably going to be a professor of Mayan culture one day. My aunt and uncle have taught me so much from their travels and from books and pictures, but they've always said that to get a real feel for a culture or civilization, it's important to see it in person, which is why I want to take a trip to Mexico. How can I properly write a report about the indigenous people of the Riviera Maya and Cancún regions if I don't go there and see it with my own eyes? And how can I ever fully know who I am if I don't see where I came from?"

"I agree," Doli added. "My parents feel the same way. I was lucky enough to grow up on a reservation surrounded by my elders and their traditions."

"Me too," said Lin. "Well, I mostly grew up in California, but I've been to China several times. My father has always been very proud of our heritage and made sure I had the opportunity to experience it for myself, not just in museums. That's part of why he is—or was—such a large donor to this school, so it would have the money to help less fortunate students"—Lin inclined her head toward Doli and me—"enjoy the same opportunity. I'm sure he wouldn't want to hear that some students weren't getting as good an education just because they didn't have the money to travel."

"So since we're doing this group project anyway," Doli continued, "we think Ana deserves to go on this trip."

"We all do," I finished. "And since Ms. Benitez is already there, we would have adult supervision the whole time. We can stay with her, provided we leave today."

I exhaled. Our pitch was perfect. I'd gone in there feeling like we were making a kind of ridiculous request, and I wouldn't have been surprised if she had just laughed in our faces. But after the rough start, it couldn't have gone better. Except that Principal Ferris's face was still full of *No*.

"Ladies," she said, "it's great that you're so fired up about your culture, but this is extremely short notice. I wouldn't have time to put through the proper paperwork. . . . I just don't think this is a good idea."

"I do," a voice said from the doorway. *Jason!* He met my eyes for a long time, then turned to his mother. "I think it's a great idea. Parents' weekend is coming up next month, and didn't you once tell me that diversity is the third most important thing that parents look for in a boarding school?"

Principal Ferris looked up at her son in surprise. "That is true," she said slowly. "However, Temple Academy is already a huge supporter of diversity initiatives."

"Yeah, but just in the school and in the local community. How cool would it be to tell the parents that we funded an independent research project in Mexico to support cultural exploration? They'd flip. It's the kind of thing they want to know would be possible for their kids. Besides, wouldn't you rather tell them about that than all the vandalism that's been going on?"

The principal looked wounded. The "vandalism" of the temple and the gym was clearly still a sore subject for her, and the temple probably reminded her of Dr. Logan.

"The school does budget for a few trips in the jet each semester, right?" I asked.

"Well, yes, I suppose," the principal said. "And all the parents have signed waivers for their children to travel abroad for educational purposes. . . ." I could see her resolve weakening.

I looked up at Jason, who stared right back at me. His eyes were intense, like he was hoping we could go just as much as we were. *He knows this is about the Brotherhood,* I realized. Even though he wasn't speaking to me, he was still trying to help—maybe because I hadn't asked him to.

"So can they go, Mom?"

After a few beats of silence, Principal Ferris nodded glumly. "I can see I'm outnumbered," she sighed.

I jumped up and hugged Doli and Lin, who were smiling from ear to ear, unlike our principal, who had that sad, far-away look in her eye again. But she quickly shook it off.

"I'll work out the details of your departure with Antonio, but I want you to understand that this won't be just a sightseeing trip, ladies. In addition to your research project, you will be required to write up an article about your experience for the Temple Academy magazine, and you'll have to present your findings at a special morning assembly. Is that understood?"

"Of course," I gushed. "We won't let you down."

I hugged Doli and Lin again and locked eyes with Jason. *Thank you,* I mouthed. But he just looked away and muttered, "I gotta go, Mom. Lots of homework. See you back at the house."

He left without another word. Even though we'd gotten what we'd come for, I felt a sharp pang of loss.

An hour later we were standing on the runway, about to board the jet. We each had a small suitcase, which Antonio had stored on board, though I'd kept one duffel bag with me containing a very special item—the vase Ixchel had made to trap the Chaos Spirits inside. It was nearly an exact copy of the vase my aunt and uncle had donated to the school, and I could almost see the emerald fixed to the top of it, glowing through the bag. That was the gem that had called the defeated bat Chaos Spirit back to the vase and trapped it inside.

"You're bringing that with us?" Lin asked.

"I have to," I said. "I can't leave it unguarded at the school. Not with Nicole and who knows who else still hanging out there."

"Fine, but if the bat gets out and we have to fight it again, you're paying for my manicures till the end of time." Though her parents had lost most of their money to a shady accountant, Lin still had the wardrobe of a starlet. She tied a white silk scarf over her head, threw on a pair of black Dior sunglasses, and climbed the steps to the jet.

Doli followed Lin, shaking her head and mumbling, "She thinks she's Audrey Hepburn or something."

I laughed and lingered on the stairs, looking out at the gate. Even though I knew it was unlikely, part of me still hoped Jason would come to see us off and wish us luck. But he was nowhere to be found. I was starting to turn away, when I saw a swish of black fur and the glimmer of green eyes emerge from the bushes. We still hadn't settled on a name for the cat, but she was ours all the same, an honorary Hunter of Chaos. She ran up and pawed at the stairs, looking at the jet and letting out plaintive meows.

"Oh, all right. I should've known you wouldn't want to be left behind." I picked her up with one hand and settled her on my shoulder. She licked my cheek with her rough tongue, and we climbed into the jet.

"The cat's coming too?" asked Doli as she settled into her seat.

I shrugged. "I don't think she'd take no for an answer. Besides, she seems to know things about the Brotherhood that we don't. I can't explain how, but maybe she'll be able to help us find what we're looking for."

"Then we should probably do her the courtesy of giving her a name," said Lin.

I stroked the cat's midnight-black fur. "I'm sure she'll eventually let me know what she wants to be called."

Suddenly the cockpit door opened and Antonio, the school's pilot, came into the cabin. He had a big smile on his face, half covered by a bushy gray beard. He slapped his large hands together. "Ladies, welcome to my pride and joy. I call her *Venezia*. It will be my honor to fly you to Mexico today."

I smiled back. "Really? Nicole made it sound like you didn't like kids being in the jet."

His face darkened at the mention of Nicole's name. "That one is a different story," he said, wagging his finger back and forth. "She is not welcome here. But you—you say you're going to meet Ms. Benitez, yes?"

"Yes," I said. I didn't want to add that we'd have to find her first.

Antonio slapped a hand over his heart and said, "It is my duty to help anyone who is a friend to Ms. Benitez." He gave me a look that made me wonder if he knew more than he let on. But if he did, he wasn't saying.

After he returned to the cockpit, the rest of us strapped into our seats, and the cat settled onto my lap. I checked my phone one last time, hoping to see a message from Jason. I'd texted him the minute we'd left Principal Ferris's office, practically falling all over myself to thank him for helping us, but he never replied.

"Has anybody heard from Shani yet?" I asked, forcing myself to put the phone down.

"No," said Doli, "and I'm worried now. I've been texting her all these messages, and she usually responds right away. Ana, you don't think she really is angry at us for letting her get kicked out of school, do you?"

I sighed and shook my head. "Honestly, at this point I hope that's all it is. But for right now, all we can do is focus on finding Ms. Benitez and my aunt and uncle. Then maybe we can make things right with Shani."

"Sounds like a plan," said Doli.

chapter 9

Ana

THE SECOND WE TOUCHED DOWN IN CANCÚN, I TURNED ON my phone and texted Jason.

We're here. Can't thank you enough.

I probably wouldn't get a response to that either, but I had to try. After Antonio pulled into a private hangar, he helped us with our bags as we climbed down the stairs.

"Girls, I have to stay with the plane, so this is as far as I can go. But if you need anything, you call me right away." He took my phone from my hand and added his number to my contact list.

"Thank you, Antonio." I shook his hand, my slender one almost disappearing in his.

He nodded seriously and said, "Be careful."

"We will," I said. I knelt down and picked up the cat, who curled around my shoulders and purred in my ear.

Antonio raised his eyebrows. "Oh no, no, no. That cat

will never make it through customs. You'll have to hide her somewhere."

I thought for a minute. "Lin, can you take her?" When Lin nodded and held out her arms, I handed over the cat and unzipped my suitcase. I pulled out a yellow raincoat. It had deep pockets inside meant to keep valuables dry. I put it on and reached for the cat. "I know you're used to traveling in style now," I whispered into her ear, "but would you mind riding inside my pocket just until we leave the airport? You're an important part of the team, and we can't afford to lose you."

To all of our surprise, the cat licked my hand and then climbed into the pocket by herself, sinking into it with a soft purr.

"Incredible!" Antonio said. "How did you get her to do that?"

I shrugged. "I asked her nicely?"

Antonio laughed. "I'll have to try that next time I ask my mother-in-law to go home, ah?" He winked.

After Antonio got back on the plane, the rest of us made our way through customs (the cat unnoticed), through the terminal, and into the blinding sunlight of Cancún. The heat felt good on my skin after the hours of air-conditioning on the jet. As soon as we reached the passenger pickup lanes outside the glass doors of the baggage claim area, we spotted a taxi stand.

"What now?" Doli asked.

"Now we get to work," I said. I fished into my backpack and pulled out three copies of a picture I'd printed out before we'd left campus. It was Ms. Benitez's faculty photo from the Temple Academy website. I handed each of the girls a copy. "Ms. Benitez must have taken a cab when she left the airport. So let's split up and show all the drivers her picture. With any luck, one of them will remember her. If none of them do, we'll go to the other terminals and ask them."

It was a long shot, I knew. But I was counting on the fact that Ms. Benitez's inner goddess made her stand out in a crowd, even when she wasn't trying to. If she had been here, I just sensed that someone would know it.

Still, when I started showing the photo around, driver after driver told me they hadn't seen her. After a while I started to lose hope. The sun was setting, and we were still no closer to finding our teacher. But Doli and Lin weren't giving up, so I couldn't either. Soon there was only one taxi left, waiting near the entrance to the airport parking garage. I rolled my suitcase up to his passenger-side window.

"Con permiso," I said. Spanish for "excuse me." I held up the picture. *"¿Recuerda usted a esta señora?"*

He leaned closer to the picture, and his eyes lit up. *"¡Sí! La lleve a Chichén Itzá hace dos dias."*

Chichén Itzá! Of course. It only made sense that a Mayan goddess would visit the famous Mayan ruins! I shrieked in excitement and told him not to move because my friends and I would be right back.

While the driver put our bags in the trunk, I piled into the backseat with Lin and Doli, and the cat crawled out of my pocket and curled up on Lin's lap. "He said he saw Ms. Benitez. He took her to Chichén Itzá two days ago."

"Chichén Itzá? That famous Mayan pyramid thing? But that's not even in Cancún—it's, like, a three-hour drive," said Lin. When Doli and I both looked at her in surprise, Lin took off her sunglasses and said, "What? I'm not just a pretty face. I know things."

Doli took out her phone and typed Chichén Itzá into the Google Maps app that Shani had installed. "Ugh, Lin's right. Guess we're in for a long drive!"

"Told you," Lin said, folding her sunglasses and slipping them into her bag.

"But why would she have gone to see an ancient Mayan ruin so far from Cancún?" I asked.

Doli shrugged. "Maybe that's where she was meeting her contacts, or maybe she found something that told her that your aunt and uncle were there."

"Maybe," I said.

By then the driver had climbed back into the front seat. He turned the key in the ignition and asked, in heavily accented English, "Where do you want to go?"

"Take us to Chichén Itzá, please," I said.

The driver reached for his keys again and turned the car back off, shaking his head. "Sorry. I can't take you there."

"Why not?" Lin asked.

He gestured to the sky, which was now a faded orange threatening to turn black. "By the time we get there, it will be closed to the public," he explained. "How old are all of you, anyway?"

We looked at one another with a hint of panic. We needed to come up with some reason for him to take us without asking so many questions.

"It doesn't matter," Lin said after a second. "We're meeting my parents there. They arrived on an earlier flight."

"Yeah," Doli added. "And there will be a huge tip in it for you if you get us to our hotel safely."

The driver seemed to like the sound of that. But he scratched at his clean-shaven face and asked, "What hotel?"

"Uh . . . just let me check the e-mail from her parents real quick." But of course there was no e-mail to check. I did a quick search on an Internet travel site for hotels near Chichén Itzá and named the first one that popped up on the list. "The Mayan Oasis Hotel."

"*Bueno,*" the driver said. He turned the key in the ignition and started driving.

We all breathed a sigh of relief and settled in.

But I couldn't relax until I checked my phone one last

time. It had been hours, and Jason still hadn't responded to my texts. Why? I knew he might not have wanted to hang out with me anymore, but I thought he at least cared about our mission. Could something have happened to him since we'd seen him in Principal Ferris's office? I couldn't help myself. I pulled up his name and typed: *R U OK?* And before I could change my mind, I hit send. Then I closed my eyes and tried to get some sleep. We had a long ride ahead of us.

Hours later I felt the taxi rumble to a stop. I cracked open my eyes. Doli had fallen asleep against the window, I was slumped against her, and Lin was slumped against me. But the cat was on the floor of the cab, pawing at the door and whining.

"*Estamos aqui,*" the driver said.

I shook Doli and Lin awake. "We're here." Doli stretched and opened the door, freeing the cat, who ran behind the nearest bush. I checked my phone to see the time, but was distracted by the sight of two text messages waiting for me. Jason had finally written back. I quickly swiped the screen to read what he had to say at last.

I'm just not sure what this is.

A few minutes later he'd added:

I need some time to think.

I sucked in my breath, feeling like I'd been shot through the heart. I knew he wasn't asking for much. But it still hurt. My eyes filled with tears.

"Hey, you all right?" Doli asked, noticing the stricken look on my face.

I nodded. "Just tired," I said. No point in getting into my romantic woes now. We had bigger things to worry about.

We climbed out of the car, and the driver lifted our bags from the trunk. Lin pulled out her wallet and handed the driver a stack of bills. Thankfully, she still got a generous monthly allowance from her parents. We'd agreed to pay her back when we could.

"*Gracias por todo,*" I said to the driver. "Thank you for everything."

Lin and Doli thanked him too. Even the cat emerged from the bushes to rub against his leg and purr. He looked around as we stood in the hotel's covered driveway. "Your parents . . . where are they?" he asked Lin.

"They're inside," she answered quickly, as if she had expected him to ask. "Don't worry about us. You have a long drive back to Cancún. You should go." She handed him another ten-dollar bill, shooing him back toward the cab.

Finally, he shoved the money into his pocket, smiled, and said good-bye, climbing back into his car. As we watched the taillights fade into the distance, Lin asked, "So are we checking in here?"

Doli huffed. "Are you crazy? We just handed that guy half our money. I doubt we have enough now to even sleep in their driveway."

Lin's face fell. "So what are we going to do?"

I smiled and whispered, "WWSD?" When I got blank looks from Doli and Lin, I said, "What Would Shani Do? My friends, it's time to go break into an ancient ruin."

chapter 10
Shani

WHEN THE MOST EXCITING THING YOU HAVE TO DO ALL DAY is watch *The Karate Kid* dubbed in Hindi, you know you've got big problems. But it was either that or stare at the walls. It was only eleven in the morning, and already I was the most bored I'd ever been in my entire life. Sonia, Dad, and Kiah had all left for work or school, and I didn't know anyone in Mumbai. Even the private tutor couldn't start until next week.

Ralph Macchio waxed on and off, though I couldn't understand what he was saying. Then the TV abruptly went black, along with the light hanging from the ceiling. Dad had warned me that power outages were pretty common here, even in the nice parts of town. Now one had taken away the only form of entertainment I had. I screamed in frustration and kicked one of the couch cushions across the room.

My father's apartment was starting to feel like a prison, except I was the only convict. *It's not fair.* I hadn't been the only one in the gym, so why was I the only one exiled to no-man's-land? I took a deep breath and let it out slowly. I knew that what had happened to me wasn't my friends' fault, and *I'd* been the one who had stopped Ana from telling Principal Ferris the truth. And I knew that, even if she had, I still would've been the only one expelled, since I was the only one caught on tape and, as Lin kept reminding me, I had a record.

But what had I really *done* to deserve this lame new life? Stopped a teacher from logging on to Facebook, and turned on some sprinklers? Even if it was just for one semester, the punishment didn't fit the crime. I had hoped I could start over, but how was I supposed to do that from here?

I walked to the window that overlooked the city far below, absentmindedly rubbing the lion on my bracelet. I glanced down at it, remembering the first time I'd transformed and how powerful I'd felt, especially because I'd been with Lin, Doli, and Ana. Amazing how quickly everything had changed. I was no longer a Temple Academy student, but was I still a Hunter? I had tried and failed to turn into a lion while the dogs were attacking me. Did that mean I couldn't do it anymore? I was almost scared of the answer, but I had to know.

I returned to the center of the living room and closed my eyes. I thought of heavy paws, running through the woods, my hair turning buttery gold. When I opened my eyes, I saw that I was on all fours. It had worked. I quickly transformed back. If Sonia or my dad came home unexpectedly, they'd have heart attacks if they found a lion in their living room. I wondered what possible good being a shape-shifter would do me in Mumbai. Did India have circuses and freak shows?

And if I wasn't actively hunting evil, would evil hunt me? Or would Anubis and his minions just leave me—and the world—alone?

I was walking around the apartment, looking at my father's and Sonia's things, when I noticed an English-language newspaper lying on the coffee table. I bent my head and read the headline of a small front-page article.

EGYPTIAN ARTIFACT FOUND FAR FROM HOME

I laughed. *That could describe me*, I thought. I read on.

Early yesterday morning workers in famed Mumbai temple Shree Siddhivinayak reported finding an artifact believed to be Egyptian in origin. Archae-ologist Dr. Joseph Penwar has identified the object as an amulet featuring an *amenta*, the symbol of the land of the dead. Local historians are puzzled as to how the artifact came to be found in this location. Authorities are investigating the possibility that it was a result of a tourist or researcher who has vis-ited both sites, or the work of a practical joker.

I stopped laughing, feeling my heart thump in my chest. The whole scenario sounded familiar. Ana had told us that Jason had found a Roman coin where it had no right to be, in a Native American temple. That coin was part of how we found out that the temple was not built by the ancient pueblo peoples as a place for worship after all. It was a meeting place for the members of several ancient civilizations— the Brotherhood of Chaos!

Did the fact that an Egyptian artifact was found in India mean that the Brotherhood was now using *this* temple as a meeting place? I had to find out. And I had to tell the other Hunters!

I ran to my room to get my cell phone so I could text Ana. But only when I had my bag in my hand did I remember: I had no cell phone. And even though I had my laptop, the Wi-Fi was off until Dad came home, and even then I'd have to sneak around to hack in, *No cell phone, no Internet, no life. I might as well just go back to bed right now.*

But then I got a grip on myself. *Hold on a minute. You can't just give up because you don't have Internet access! That would be pathetic.* My dad had told me the other night that I was more than these computer screens, and he was right. I could figure this out on my own. Maybe by the time I did, I'd have a Wi-Fi signal again and some interesting new info for my friends. I hoped so, because then it would mean that my banishment had been worthwhile. I put my bag over my shoulder, grabbed my copy of the key, and left the apartment.

I got to the sidewalk and tried to remember what I could. I had been to Mumbai before with my parents, but the last time had been years ago—before the divorce, before Sonia, and definitely before Mumbai-Lin. Nothing looked the same. But I had paid attention to the route the driver had taken when he'd brought me from the airport. There had been a picture of the temple in the newspaper, and I was pretty sure I had passed it on our way to the apartment. I would follow the same path in reverse to get me into town.

As I made my way to the busiest part of the city, I realized that Mumbai was total Brotherhood bait. The place was already the definition of chaos, with crazy traffic going in every direction, rickshaws weaving between huge buses and speeding cars, and an oppressive heat threatening to bake everyone where they stood. That must have been why everyone moved so fast here. They were afraid they would melt if they stood still.

I kept walking until I saw the colorfully painted aluminum structures that told me I was nearing the poorer section of town. Everywhere I looked, someone was selling something— flowers, vegetables, deep-fried bread. When I stopped to look around, three small children ran up to me, saying something excitedly in Hindi and holding out their hands. Their clothes were torn and dirty, and they looked like they hadn't eaten a decent meal in weeks. I gave them every bit of loose change I had in my pocket, even though it was American money. They shouted happily as they stared at the shiny new coins in their hands, and then tore down the street.

For a second I smiled. But as I looked around at the muddy roads and overcrowded streets, my smile faded. What was life like for these children? All at once I felt ashamed for complaining about being bored as I sat in my father's beautiful luxury apartment with a refrigerator full of food and lush carpet under my feet. I always got on Lin about acting like a privileged jerk. It felt terrible to realize that I'd been acting like one too.

While I was thinking all of this, I must have taken a wrong turn. I passed by a stall selling scarves and saris that I could have sworn I had already passed twice before. I realized with a sinking feeling that I was going around in circles, and now I was so hopelessly lost that I didn't even know if I could find my way back to the apartment. If only I had my smartphone. Having GPS means never having to say, "I'm lost."

I was standing at a street corner with sweat pouring down my back, desperately trying to get my bearings, when I heard a familiar voice yell in English, "Oh-Em-GEE. It's YOU!"

I closed my eyes and cursed my luck. *Please don't be her, please don't be her. . . .* I turned around, and sure enough, there she was: Kiah in her maroon-and-white uniform, surrounded by a pack of girls in identical outfits and with identical mean grins on their faces. They'd just emerged from an alleyway and were watching me with grim satisfaction.

"Is that her?" one of them asked Kiah with a giggle. When Kiah nodded, the girl added, "I see what you mean" and started laughing. When she opened her mouth, I noticed that her two front teeth overlapped, almost as if they were hugging.

Finally Kiah stepped toward me and crossed her arms. "So what is my new criminal stepsister doing out here?" she asked. "Mugging little children? Or perhaps a little light bank robbery is more your thing? Or maybe"—she got right up in my face while her friends moved in closer—"you just came out here to accuse me of attacking you again."

I gasped. She couldn't have heard that conversation with Dad this morning. Kiah had still been in bed, snoring away, I was sure of it.

I longed to give Kiah one of the trademark comebacks that I would have used on Nicole in a heartbeat. But then, I'd never actually been afraid that Nicole would hurt me the way Kiah had. I had also never been this outnumbered. Her friends slowly surrounded me, lowering their heads and eyeing me in a way that felt familiar in the worst way possible. I had to make a move now before something bad happened.

I pushed my way between two of the smaller girls and mumbled, "Just leave me alone, all right?" I darted into the nearest alley, walking as quickly as I could, and then emerging onto a main street lined with cars.

The temple was several stories high, and I'd hoped maybe I could see it from there, but all I could see were the tin roofs and columns of smoke rising from exhaust pipes. I was just about to pick a direction and go with it, when I heard a menacing growl right behind me.

I spun around to find a pack of feral dogs, snarling and baring their long jagged teeth at me. One of them had a long scar across the top of its head where the hair had stopped growing. *I knew that scar!* These were the dogs that had attacked me last night.

Are these dogs . . . Kiah's friends? The dog with the scar snapped at me, my heart leaped into my throat, and I took off running. "Help!" I shouted as I ran. But no one else seemed to think my being chased by bloodthirsty dogs was any of their business. Was it possible that they couldn't see them?

As I ran, I desperately tried to place the landmarks. But everything was starting to look the same. And that river in the distance, had that been on my left or my right on the way to the apartment? Or had I seen it at all? I had no idea.

What I did know was that the dogs were gaining on me. I stopped to swerve around a man pulling a rickshaw behind him, and one of the dogs took the opportunity to lunge at me. Its teeth caught the edge of my T-shirt and ripped right through it. The close call was enough to get me sprinting at top speed. I might not have been good enough for the tennis team, but if Coach Connolly could have seen me, she would have signed me up for track on the spot.

The dogs stayed right on my tail, though. One of them

even swiped at my foot as I ran, nearly tripping me. If I fell now, I would be done for.

Finally I turned a corner onto Dadar Phool Gali. I remembered it instantly from when I was a kid. The street was filled with vendors selling every kind of flower I could imagine. The smell of yellow and orange marigolds hung heavily in the air, and there were people milling around everywhere, haggling with the vendors. *Now's my chance,* I thought. There were so many scents here, maybe the dogs would find it too hard to pick out mine. All I had to do was find a place to hide until they gave up and went on their way.

I burst through the crowd, vendors' startled yells fading away as I cut through the throng, my black T-shirt and denim jeans standing out against the sea of red and purple saris. I passed stands selling roasting meat and balls of rice covered in thick syrup. The old women working the stands reached out to me, encouraging me to buy. Somewhere in the crowd I lost the dogs, but I kept moving, checking behind me every few minutes to see if they had caught up again. Finally an old man moved into my path, blocking my way. By then I was panting for breath and my legs were burning. I looked up at the man, and he flashed me a kind smile. I realized that he was holding out a cup to me, and I inhaled the delicious smell of vanilla chai. I was so thirsty, I almost grabbed the cup, but then I remembered that I had absolutely no money on me. I'd given it all away to the children. I backed away from him and turned my jeans pockets inside out so he could see what I had to offer—a whole lot of nothing. The man smiled serenely and pushed the cup into my hands.

Just then I heard a vicious growl, and I knew—the dogs had found me. I turned and saw the members of the pack weaving through the crowd of people, never taking their eyes off me. *Can anyone else see them?* The fur on their backs stuck straight up, and as they got closer, their growls grew more intense, hungrier. But at the last moment the man who'd given me the tea slid between the dogs and me. He leaned over and growled back at them.

Did he really just do that? For a moment I considered the possibility that I was suffering from heatstroke and was imagining the whole thing. The man unleashed a torrent of Hindi on the dogs in a voice that sounded many years younger than he must have been. Even more amazing, at the man's words the dogs whined and backed away, lowering their snouts and tucking their tails between their legs. They turned and scampered back into the maze of stalls, disappearing into the crowd.

"How did you do that?" I cried, my eyes practically popping out of my head. "Thank you! You saved my life." But the tea seller didn't respond. He merely cleared his throat as if all he'd done was shoo away some pesky mosquitoes. Then he pressed his hands against mine and lifted the cup toward my mouth. He wanted me to drink the tea. "But I . . . I can't pay you," I said, willing him to understand me. "I have no money."

He nodded and pushed at the cup again. I did as he wanted, taking a slow sip of the delicious tea. "Thank you," I said again, wishing I knew how to say that in Hindi.

"Finish it," he said suddenly. "It will give you sustenance."

"You speak English?" I exclaimed, unable to hide my surprise.

"I speak many languages," he answered. He waited for me to finish the tea and then took back the cup.

I bowed low and said, "Thank you again. I owe you my life."

This time he said nothing, just inclined his head as if to say, *You're welcome,* and watched me walk away. Right ahead of me I could see the temple I'd been searching for all day. I joined the line forming outside it, feeling that my luck was finally changing.

But just before I entered the temple, I glanced back toward the tea seller's stall. He remained there, watching me, his kind eyes filled with worry.

chapter 11

Ana

THE DRIZZLE THAT HAD BEGUN WHEN WE'D GOTTEN OUT of the cab had turned into a monsoon. At least it felt that way as the rain soaked every inch of clothes that weren't covered by my raincoat. But just before midnight we reached our destination. On the other side of a low metal gate, Chichén Itzá rose steeply into the sky, rain battering its ancient steps.

The chains on the gates and the high walls might have stopped three teenage girls, but once we'd transformed into three large cats—and one small black one—the barriers barely ranked as obstacles. We left our belongings under a tree and easily scaled the wall after prowling along its edge until we found a soft place to land inside the grounds. I lifted my nose, sniffing the air and hoping to catch Ms. Benitez's scent, but the heavy rain made it hard to smell anything.

I stood at the foot of the stairs, looking up at the small structure above the steps, dark and mysterious against the starlit sky. I remembered Uncle Mec telling me that the Mayans had built ninety-one steps on each of the four sides. Those plus the top platform equaled 365, the number of days in a year. To the Mayans there was both magic and order in numbers. I ran up the steps in front of me, hoping to find a clue in the small room at the top, but there was nothing inside. And when I came back out and looked at the view from there, I remembered that Chichén Itzá was more than just the structure I stood on now, El Castillo. It was a city of ruins, one whose people had abandoned it one day for some unknown reason. A city where ritual sacrifices had taken place to satisfy the gods of rain, who seemed to be alive and well. As the distant clouds above continued to pour over the ruins, I could feel the whole area pulsing with power. But how were we supposed to find Ms. Benitez?

As I was about to descend the stairs, I spotted a figure carved into the outside wall. My heart jumped into my throat as I realized it was a stylized cat, just like the one I'd seen on the vases outside the temple at school. This carving was old. It had been worn away by time and rain, but it was still obvious that it had been here even before these structures had become ruins.

A year ago I might have written the symbol off as just another sign that the Mayans, along with many other ancient peoples, revered cats. But I knew now that this symbol indicated the presence of the Brotherhood of Chaos. I hissed at it and backed away, then hurried down the stairs, feeling a growing sense of dark magic simmering all around us. On my way back to the others, I noticed a waxy flyer on the ground. I pawed at it, but it sank deeper into the mud under my weight. I needed human hands. I transformed back into my human form and picked up the flyer. The others changed too, and Doli asked, "What is it?"

"It's a tourist guide," I answered, "and there's a map on the back."

"Great," Lin said. "Does it have a little red arrow on it anywhere that says, 'Ms. Benitez is here'?"

I grunted. "I wish. We're just going to have to look around. If she's here, maybe we'll feel her presence."

I dropped the map, and we transformed back into our cat selves. But after searching all the nearby ruins and coming up empty, we were all getting discouraged. Even the black cat seemed tired, listlessly pawing at the ground. Inside one of the large stone enclosures, we collapsed onto our haunches and took a break.

My paws are killing me, Lin complained, *and I'm starving.* She chuffed at us and shook her huge head, spraying water from her striped coat.

Hey! Watch that, Doli said.

Like it matters, I broke in. *We're all soaked to the bone anyway.*

We were getting tired and cranky, and if I'm being honest,

we were more than a little scared. *What was I thinking, bringing us out here?* I wondered. Maybe I'd made a huge mistake.

Of course, I'd forgotten that in our cat forms, the others could hear my thoughts. Lin pounced right away. *Good question,* she responded. *What if Ms. Benitez isn't even here? For all you know she's sipping margaritas back at some other hotel, where she's warm . . . and dry!* Lin shivered again, sending more sprays of water into the air.

No, I insisted. *She wouldn't do that. Not when she knows my aunt and uncle could be in danger.*

Don't be so naive, Lin argued. *I know you think it's just me, but everyone is a little selfish, deep down.*

Even ancient Mayan gods? Doli asked.

Especially gods! Haven't you ever read Greek mythology? Ares killed Adonis just because he wanted Aphrodite for himself. Calypso trapped guys on her island for years because she was bored and lonely. And don't even get me started on—

Guys! The cat—she's leaving, I interrupted. We all turned to watch as the sleek black cat sped up the stairs of the chamber and paused at the doorway. She scratched at the ground and sniffed the dirt, then turned her luminous green eyes on us.

I think she's telling us she knows where to go, I said. *This is the same thing that happened when she led us to the entrance of the temple on campus. Remember, Doli?*

I remember.

I swished my heavy tail. *Let's follow her.*

We all took off running after the cat. If I hadn't been in jaguar form, it would have been almost impossible to keep an eye on her, since she blended into the shadows so well. But she was leading us on a path straight back to El Castillo. Moments later we found ourselves at the foot of the giant pyramid, right where we had started.

This can't be right, I said. *I checked this already, and it was empty.*

We didn't know about the temple's secret entrance back on campus either, though, Doli reminded me. *Maybe the cat knows something we don't.*

She'd better, Lin added. *If this isn't it, I'm heading back to that hotel and calling my father.*

Sure enough, instead of climbing, as I had done, the cat padded around to the left side of the pyramid, the one facing the expanse of trees. There, not far from the serpent head statue at the base of the stairs, was a door—one that hadn't appeared on any map I'd ever seen—camouflaged into the rock. The cat pawed it, yowling and looking back at us. Instinctually I roared along with her. Soon Lin and Doli joined in, our roars matched only by the pounding of the rain. Slowly the door crept open just enough for us to see a dim light beckoning us inside. I leaned against the door. It budged a little, but it was heavy. *Lin, Doli, I need your help,* I called.

They came right away, and we each pressed our muscular

bodies against the door until finally it ground open and emitted more of that unnatural light. From deep inside we heard voices shouting and felt a surge of power buzzing all around us. I looked at my friends. *She's here!* We ran in without another thought.

At the bottom of the stairs we stopped to look at the walls around us. The décor was horrifyingly familiar. The odd light I had noticed from outside came from torches fitted into sconces mounted on the walls—fires that no human hand had lit. The flames licking at the carvings in the wall made the carvings look even more disturbing. Bat-winged demons with sharpened claws descended on a pride of lions. Armies of skeletons armed with spears marched toward cornered tigers. What looked like panthers cowered in fear before gigantic serpents. And horrible-looking monkey creatures leered at a group of suffering jaguars.

It looks just like the hall of suffering from the last temple, I said. *We must be in another temple of the Brotherhood of Chaos!*

Doli shook her great puma head. *This one is worse.*

Why do you say that? Lin asked, her eyes darting around the room.

Because in the last one everyone was fair game for torture. But most of these *picture demons tormenting and killing big cats—like us.*

Look away, I ordered immediately. *It's just meant to scare us off. Ms. Benitez needs us.*

Just then we heard a woman scream. As one, we took off in the direction of her voice, the black cat racing along behind us.

We came to another set of stairs that spiraled down into what should have been darkness, but instead the staircase was lit with the glow of magic. It was way too narrow for us to go down as cats, so we transformed back into our human selves and descended the stairs. When we reached the bottom, we found her: Ixchel, her arms raised against a tall man wearing a bird-beak mask and carrying a wooden shield. The air hummed with magic, and Ixchel's deep purple eyes flashed with power, but I could tell she was tired. *How long has she been fighting? Days?*

"You have come too soon," Ixchel shouted at the man in that voice that sounded like many and one at the same time. "The End Times are not yet upon us." She sent a bolt of white light soaring at her enemy, but he blocked it with his shield and it bounced off harmlessly.

"You are wrong," he said. "The balance of good and evil has shifted, and the earth cries out for me. Do not get in my way!" He swung his ax at her, and she backed out of its path.

I stared at the man, my mind exploding with shock. I had seen him before. Not the real-life being, but statues and drawings of him. Aunt Teppy had taken me once to the Cleveland Museum of Art to see an exhibit about mythical creatures of the ancient world. I'd stood before a colorful drawing of him for the longest time, trying to decide if he was good or bad. The Aztecs had thought he was the god of wind, but the Mayans had called him by another name—one that meant "the feathered serpent."

"It's Quetzalcoatl!" I shouted. "He's another Mayan god."

"He's not on our side, I take it," said Lin.

I sighed. "Not exactly. He represents both good and evil, but he's only supposed to return to earth when the world is coming to an end. If he's here, it's because Anubis convinced him that the battle between good and evil was almost over and that Anubis was going to win. Quetzalcoatl has come to help end things."

"But he looks like a regular man," Doli said, confused.

"That isn't his true form."

Lin cringed. "I hate to ask, but what is his true form?"

"You don't want to know."

As we watched, Quetzalcoatl backed Ixchel into a corner. He shot a bolt of magic at Ixchel, and she went flying into the wall, hit it with a sickening thud, and slid to the floor.

"We have to help her!" I yelled. I put Quetzalcoatl in my sights and thought of him not as a man or a god or even a feathered serpent—but as dinner. A juicy capybara, maybe, that I spotted through dense forest trees. I licked my muzzle, already salivating at the thought of taking down my prey. Without another sound I charged Quetzalcoatl. Lin and Doli were right behind me. Together we leaped onto the warrior's back, tackling him to the floor. I snapped at the back of his neck, catching the salty taste of his skin, which felt surprisingly more like the leathery hide of a snake. But the acrid smell of fear seeped from him in pungent waves like a man.

He let out a cry and rolled away from us, but Doli lunged for him, letting out a long "RAWWWR!" She snagged his thigh and calf with her long sharp claws, opening up two punishing wounds, and his skin flapped down like a banana peel. Somehow he got to his feet and limped away into a nearby chamber, squealing in terror and leaving a trail of blood behind him. It wasn't enough to stop him for good, I knew—he was a god, after all—but Doli had bought us precious time.

I transformed again, ran to Ixchel, and knelt by her side. Before my eyes Ixchel's snake headpiece and plum-colored eyes disappeared and were replaced by Ms. Benitez's dark brown eyes. Her matching hair was plastered to her sweat-drenched face. Her normally creamy tan complexion was pale and splotchy, the blood beneath her skin so near the surface. She was breathing hard, and her eyes rolled in their sockets as though she were a spooked horse. Slowly she brought them under control, clearly struggling to focus. Finally she saw my face. "Ana! I thought I might never see you again in this life. How did you find me?"

"We weren't sure we'd ever see you again either," Doli said. "When we found out that you had never checked in at the hotel, we thought something awful had happened. I guess we were right."

"I shouldn't have come to Chichén Itzá on my own," she agreed.

"Why did you?" Lin asked.

"When I landed in Cancún, I felt something pulling me to Chichén Itzá. When I got here, I realized that the power I'd felt was dark magic. Anubis had brought Quetzalcoatl back to life before his time in order for Quetzalcoatl to join the Brotherhood of Chaos."

I sucked in my breath. It all made sense. Anubis was bringing more gods to life in order to build the strength of the Brotherhood of Chaos. If he was successful in getting enough of them together, the Wildcats wouldn't stand a chance against them, and the modern world would be thrown into chaos. In my mind I pictured raging forest fires, tsunamis, senseless wars. . . . In other words, hell on earth. "But why would he choose Quetzalcoatl?" I replied, my voice straining. "My aunt and uncle told me that Quetzalcoatl wasn't all evil. He represented knowledge and wisdom."

"That's true, Ana," Ms. Benitez said, getting to her feet and dusting herself off. "But power can be corrupted. Quetzalcoatl has been waiting centuries for his moment to take center stage at the end of days, which is his destined role. Anubis has offered to end his wait."

"So Lin was right," I said. "Gods *can* be selfish."

Ms. Benitez nodded. "Yes, they can. And Anubis knows it. He will use his knowledge of their deepest desires to rebuild the Brotherhood and restore its former power."

"Not if we have anything to say about it," I said.

Ms. Benitez reached out and cupped my cheek. "Brave girls."

Just then I heard a hissing sound like air being let out of a hundred tires. I spun around to see a huge green serpent slithering into the room from the hidden chamber where Quetzalcoatl had retreated after Doli's attack. The snake had red and green feathers sprouting from his head like a Mohawk, and his eyes were solid white. If he had been hurt by our attack moments before, it didn't show. He radiated power.

Instinctually I transformed into my jaguar guise and snarled at this new enemy.

H-his t-true form? Lin stammered, backing away.

True form, I confirmed.

Ms. Benitez shimmered in front of us, turning back into the Mayan goddess of war. As Ixchel, she seemed to gain a foot of height, and a coiled green snake writhed menacingly on top of her head, only adding to the effect. Her sweaty, blotched skin disappeared beneath Ixchel's smooth brown complexion. She wore a bold blue-and-red skirt of heavy cloth, a band of blue fabric over her chest, and a necklace of light blue stones around her neck. Her purple eyes, glowing with a magic so pure that it almost hurt to look at them, surveyed all with a calm confidence I wished I had. Doli, who had remained a human just long enough to check her own wounds, now turned into a puma and stood by Ixchel's side. Soon Lin and I joined the line, facing down this new foe as the Hunters of Chaos. "Wildcats," Ixchel whispered. "Listen with your eyes."

At first I didn't know what she meant, but then the scene in front of me vanished, and instead I saw a vision of us dividing and conquering, attacking Quetzalcoatl in a way he wouldn't be expecting. *On my word,* Ixchel's voice whispered into my mind. The vision dissipated, and I looked at my fellow Wildcats. The knowing looks in their eyes told me they'd had the same vision. Ixchel's powers never ceased to amaze me.

We waited until he got close enough for us to smell his foul breath, then Ixchel yelled, "NOW!" Just like in the vision, we darted to his side instead of charging him head-on, while Ixchel let out a blast of power that sent the serpent slithering backward. He swung his enormous head to the left and right, hissing in frustration. *He can't see us,* I realized. Ixchel's blast had temporarily blinded him. By the time he could see again, we were on all sides of him, and we attacked as one. He turned his head and spotted Lin about to pounce, so he whipped his tail, sending her flying into the stone wall by the stairs. She emitted a strangled cry that seemed like it had been torn from her throat. She rolled onto her side, and I saw a wet patch of blood where her temple had connected with the wall.

Doli bounded over the serpent's whipping tail, landed on the upper part of his body, and sunk her teeth into his neck. He hissed in pain and rolled over, pinning Doli beneath him.

We must draw him away from her, or she'll be crushed, Ixchel said.

I looked around the room, searching for a weapon I could use against the giant snake. Finally I spotted a thin stone pillar that seemed to be the only thing holding up one of the chambers in the back. *I know what to do,* I told her. *Shine your light on me to draw his attention.*

Ixchel looked at me with her unearthly eyes and raised her hand, speaking a few words in an ancient Mayan language. Soon I was awash in a pure white glow. The snake's eyes were drawn to me. He moved away from Doli, who limped over to Lin and nudged her. Meanwhile, I held the snake's gaze and stood right in front of the pillar.

I roared in his face, baring my teeth and daring him to come for me. From zoology class, I knew that all snakes strike the same way. They rear back and snap forward with such speed and force that most of their prey don't even realize they've been struck. But I was waiting for him. As he reared back, I sank onto my haunches, feeling my muscles tighten, ready to spring. And just before his head snapped forward, I leaped to the side, so that instead of devouring me, he crashed into the pillar. The pillar disintegrated on impact, sending the rock wall that had been held back by the thin support beam crashing down onto the snake's head. Within seconds his entire body was buried.

All the adrenaline I had built up left me in a blur, and I started to shake. I looked down and realized that I was human once more. I raised myself onto my forearms and looked into the eyes of the tiger and the puma across the room. As I watched, the puma's short sandy coat became a flowing mane of ink-black hair, its haunches became long brown legs, and its round yellow eyes gave way to the brown almond-shaped eyes of my friend Doli. Lin transformed too, letting go of the tiger and resuming her usual delicate beauty.

"That was brilliant!" Doli cried, running over to me.

"Brilliant and insane," Lin added. "Are you crazy? He could have killed you."

I let out a nervous laugh. "He was pretty much trying to do that anyway, right? I had to do something to make him stop. Anyway, it worked. It's over. So what do we do now, boss lady?" I said with a wink.

Doli shook her head with a rueful smile. "First thing is we get you to stop calling me that. It's bad enough I can't break Shani of the habit."

"Nope," Lin said. "First thing we do is get out of here! I don't know about you guys, but I need a taco. Like, now!"

At the mere mention of food, my stomach grumbled loudly. I leaned on my side and pressed my hand to my stomach as if trying to calm a wild animal. "Food sounds good to me," I said, still trying to slow my breathing. "But then"—I looked at Ms. Benitez—"we can keep looking for my aunt and uncle, right?"

"Girls," Ms. Benitez said, remaining next to the fall of stones. "I cannot go with you."

"What?" Lin asked, looking at Ms. Benitez as if she had truly lost her mind. "What do you mean? We came all this way to rescue you."

"And you have," Ms. Benitez said. "I'm so grateful for that. But if I leave now, Quetzalcoatl may rise again and prove to be a powerful ally to Anubis. I can make sure that doesn't happen, but to do so I have to perform a complicated spell as Ixchel. I must stay here for a few days to make sure Quetzalcoatl is gone for good."

Lin nodded limply, too tired to argue.

Ms. Benitez turned to me and said, "Ana, I am so sorry that I didn't make any progress finding your aunt and uncle. I really thought whatever force was pulling me here may have pulled them as well. But I was wrong."

"That's all right," I said. "I'm glad they weren't here. If they had been, Quetzalcoatl could've attacked them, too, and there's no way they would've been prepared for that. Plus," I added softly, "I was wrong about something too."

I told her about the fake phone call that I'd thought was from my aunt but was really just a ploy to lure us to the gym. I told her how Shani had saved us and gotten expelled and shipped off to Mumbai for her troubles. "I should never have gone to the gym, but my aunt told me she wanted to have it out with me once and for all," I told her tearfully. "I had to know for sure whether it was her."

"Dear Ana," said Ms. Benitez gently, "I am positive that was just one of Anubis's tricks. Your aunt loves you tremendously and would never speak to you that way. Trust that from now on. Anubis may try to use her against you again in the future. But if you hold on to what you know in your heart is true, he won't succeed."

Somehow she always knew exactly what to say. I knew deep down that she was right—I guess I'd known it all along— but sometimes you just need to hear the words out loud. I wiped away my tears and hugged her.

After she pulled away, Ms. Benitez looked at Lin and Doli. "I'm sorry I can't be of more help. I hope you understand why I have to stay."

Doli nodded. "It's okay, Ms. Benitez. We'll just go back to Cancún and look for Ana's aunt and uncle on our own. If we don't find them, we'll go back to school and wait to hear from you."

Ms. Benitez started to speak, but suddenly her eyes turned a dark plum color, and she lifted her gaze to the ceiling. "Wait. You cannot go to Cancún!" she whispered intensely.

I frowned. "Why not?"

"Can you not feel it?"

I stopped to focus on my body. Now that she had mentioned it, I did feel a tingling in my spine, sort of like I had the very first time the jaguar and I had become one.

Lin's eyes widened and she slapped at her back as if there were a hive of bees buzzing on her shoulder. "I sure feel it! What is this?" she cried, clearly freaked out.

"It is the call of your sister cat. You must go to Mumbai tonight," Ixchel insisted. "Shani needs you!"

chapter 12
Shani

THE LINE TO ENTER THE TEMPLE MOVED QUICKLY. I WAS grateful for that, since the man who'd given me the tea was still watching with concern from his stall. Before I was allowed in, a guard patted me down and had me pass through a metal detector. Too bad none of the things I was afraid of could be kept out by a metal detector. I wondered if maybe entering the temple alone was a bad idea. I was used to having the other Wildcats as backup in case anything bad happened. But they were all miles and miles away. I had to handle this one on my own.

Once I got inside, I felt silly for having been nervous. I didn't see any sign of the Brotherhood at all. The lobby was filled with flowers and soft candlelight. A man with bright orange cloth wrapped around his body instructed people to remove their shoes and place them in a stand of cubbyholes like those you would see in a bowling alley. I tiptoed past him, hoping I could keep my shoes on. These days I never knew when I'd have to run.

Tour groups clustered around their guides, who whispered in various languages what each relic and fountain meant to the culture. A man wearing an AUSSIE AND PROUD T-shirt tried to take a picture, but a guard rushed over and pointed to a sign expressly forbidding cameras or laptops, in addition to loud talking, gum chewing, or inappropriate clothing, whatever that meant. The guard directed the tourist over to a row of lockers, where he could turn in his camera or leave. *Guess it's a good thing I don't have anything on me*, I thought. For once, not having my usual techno gadgets worked in my favor.

While most people gravitated toward the large statue of Shree Ganesh, the destroyer of obstacles, who looked like a large red elephant, my eye wandered to a small glowing chamber off to the side of the main temple, separated from it by a metal gate. I walked in to find myself alone with a single statue. I didn't know much about Hindu gods, but I was sure I had seen this one before. He had long hair piled on top of his head and sleepy, half-open eyes. He sat cross-legged with one hand on his knee and the other raised, his palm facing me. His skin was a soft green, and he had a calm, knowing look on his face. As I moved through the room, his eyes seemed to follow me. I looked at his forehead and was startled to see a third eye there.

"That's Shiva," a girl whispered to me. "He's the destroyer of worlds."

I turned to look at her, startled to find someone standing next to me. I had been completely alone just a second ago. Where had she come from? I noted her dark skin and thin frame. She smiled, and suddenly she looked familiar. Hadn't Kiah's friend, the one who'd giggled at me earlier, had two front teeth that overlapped like this girl's? Was it possible she had trailed me here?

"How did you know I spoke English?" I asked.

She pointed to my feet. "Those sneakers. Sure sign of an American."

I looked down and winced, wondering if it was disrespectful to wear my Chuck Taylors into a temple. She was barefoot, which is why I hadn't heard her enter the room. "Actually, I'm from Egypt," I told her, "but I've been going to school in America."

The girl sniffed. "It shows."

Huh, I thought. *That was definitely* not *a compliment.* The old me would have immediately tried to find a way to cyber-sabotage her. But look where that kind of thinking had gotten me. Instead I said, "So, destroyer of worlds, huh? Sounds pretty scary," hoping to change the subject.

The girl shrugged and replied, "He's not all bad."

I eyed her with one raised eyebrow. "How can a destroyer of the world be *good*?"

"Easy," she said. "If that world has become corrupt, then destroying it and transforming it into something new isn't a bad thing." She gave me a mysterious smile and padded out of the room.

When I turned back to the statue, I froze. The arm that had been raised toward me was now folded in its lap. *What the . . .* Was I hallucinating again? Was I awake? I backed out of the room until my back pressed against the gate. I didn't want to take my eyes off Shiva in case he moved again, but I did, just long enough to see that the gate I'd come through moments before was now closed and padlocked. *Did someone lock me in here by accident?* Or had this been the work of the girl who'd just left—her way of punishing me for being the tacky American she thought I was? Either way, I was trapped!

"HELP!" I yelled, at the risk of disrespecting the temple. If someone had locked me in here, then the temple didn't have much respect for me. I tried to crane my head so I could peer into the main temple. There was no sign of the girl I had spoken to. It was as if she had vanished into thin air. Meanwhile there were people everywhere—guards, tourists, worshippers from Mumbai—but none of them seemed to hear me screaming at the top of my lungs and rattling the padlocked gate. My heart started to beat wildly in my chest. Something wasn't right. Not right at all. I backed away from the gate, suddenly sure that this had Anubis written all over it.

Then I heard a screech from the ceiling and my stomach clenched. *No! It couldn't be. . . .* How would the Chaos Spirits have found me here? Unless they had been following me all along?

I looked up just in time to see an eagle zooming toward me, its razor-sharp talons reaching for my face. I wanted to scream, to run, but I was frozen in place. For a moment time crept by, like this was all happening in slow motion. Fifteen feet away, the eagle's murderous yellow eyes, large as quarters, burned into me. Ten feet away, its yellow claws and curved black talons, like the glistening horns of a raging bull, reached out for me. Five feet away, I stood transfixed as my own death approached. . . .

But at the last second I thought, *What are you doing? MOVE!* I ducked a split second before the crushing talons could tear the flesh right off my face. The eagle, missing me by mere inches, crashed into the metal gate with a *clang!* It dropped to the floor, giving me just enough time to transform into a lion.

Shape-shifting in the temple was probably a big-time faux pas, but I had no choice. The strange thing was that I barely had to try to transform. It came naturally. Either I was just getting better at it, or transforming was easier in a place of spiritual power.

Whatever the reason, I was glad because the eagles were multiplying faster than I could count. They filled up the room, perching on the windowsill, on top of the statue, clinging to the gate. . . . Their scent—a mix of smoke and something rancid—invaded my nostrils. They weren't attacking yet. They were showing me they could take their time with me, that I was hopelessly outnumbered. My whole body quaked, and I felt tears leak from my eyes and dampen the fur on my face. I had never been so scared in my whole life.

But then, unexpectedly, my fear turned to anger. *I am a freaking Wildcat!* If I was going to go down, I could at least go down fighting. I scratched my own claws against the floor and let out a queen-of-the-jungle lion roar. *Bring it on, bird-brains!* In a flash I was on the nearest eagle, rearing up on my hind legs and crushing it with my weight. I trapped its wings under my paws and clamped my jaws around its neck, and shook it until it snapped. That seemed to animate the rest of the eagles, who all took flight at once, battering me with their huge wings and pecking me with their beaks. One rammed me from the side, knocking me onto my back, while another landed right on my soft belly and dug its talons in. The pain was so intense that I yowled. But then I slammed my heavy paw into the bird, dislodging it from my stomach and shattering its beak in three places.

I got to my feet, feeling my blood seep out of fresh wounds and onto the floor. At least this way they couldn't gut me. But they swooped in over and over, clawing and scratching at my head and back. I kept up the fight for as long as I could, but my breathing was coming in shallow gasps, and I was missing patches of fur where the eagles had ripped it out by the roots. Eventually they outnumbered me by so many, I couldn't tell one eagle from another. The room seemed to be filled with brown feathers, glistening talons, and yellow beaks. I was bringing down a bird or two at a time, but when they decided to go in for the kill, it would be easy. *Oh my God!* I thought. *I'm actually going to die here!*

I wondered if Doli, Ana, and Lin would feel it somehow. I hoped so. Otherwise, my dad would never know what happened to me, and he didn't deserve that. I hoped he wouldn't be too upset at this final screwup of mine—coming to the temple alone. Regrets tumbled through my head. *I wish I'd been nicer. I wish I'd tried harder. I wish I had told my mom that I loved her. I wish I'd helped Ana find her aunt and uncle. . . .*

Thinking of my friends and the mission we had been charged with made me want to keep fighting. I opened my eyes, looking for a weapon, anything I could use to even the odds a little. That was when I spotted a glowing hole in the floor beside the statue of Shiva. I was positive it hadn't been there earlier, but it was there now. Maybe the temple gods were trying to help me.

I struggled to my feet and ran with everything I had toward that hole in the floor. I felt an eagle's talon shred a tear along my spine, but I didn't stop. I couldn't. Now, diving into a magically appearing hole in a temple floor would probably not be a good idea to some people—or most people—but for me at that moment, it was the only choice I had if I wanted to live to fight another day. Dying was not an option—I had to get out of there alive!

Finally I reached the hole and saw a set of stairs leading down beneath the temple. I didn't think twice. I galloped down the stairs, hearing the eagles beat their wings uselessly against the floor above. Some force was keeping them at bay. When I reached the bottom, I collapsed, drinking in deep breaths. But only a second or two passed before a pair of rough hands with long nails grabbed me by my neck and threw me across the room—hard.

I saw stars and let out a whimper. My back felt like it was on fire, and blood oozed from a dozen wounds all over my body. If the eagles hadn't been able to come down here, then who had grabbed me? I slowly opened my eyes and stumbled to my feet, hissing in pain. All around me were wire bars. I was in a cage! Beyond the bars was a small room, lit by torches that filled the place with a cloying heat. I could see the engravings on the walls, some of them wooden panels—giant serpents swallowing men whole, people being stabbed with pitchforks by gleeful little pixie demons, pushing them off a cliff into the flames below. . . . And words in many languages were etched deep into the walls, some stained with blood. And just beyond the stairs, half-hidden in shadow . . .

A wooden throne sitting atop an altar of white stones and dark wood. *No, not stones,* I thought, focusing my eyes. Human skulls and bones.

No, no, no, no . . . , I cried in my head, pawing at the bars. I was in a temple that belonged to the Brotherhood of

Chaos. How could I have been so stupid? All the signs had been there—the artifact found in the wrong place, the temple already endowed with spiritual power. . . . What had I been trying to prove by coming here alone, just to confirm what was so obvious? I'd walked right into their trap!

I had gotten myself into this mess, and now my only hope was to get rescued. I didn't know if the others would be able to hear me from so far away, especially if they were in their human forms right now, but I had to try. *Doli, Ana, Lin, Ixchel . . . HELP!*

I could smell the rancid scent of rotting flesh. Behind me I heard metal clinking and something locking into place, like a key being turned. I spun to see what it was—hoping against hope that I wasn't about to see what I thought I was going to see. But there, in all his evil glory, was a creature that had haunted my dreams for weeks before I'd gotten to school—and then had appeared in the Brotherhood's HQ beneath Temple. The clawed feet of a beast, the muscular legs and broad dark chest of a man wrapped in filthy gauze strips, and the head of a jackal wearing a glimmering Egyptian head dress. *Anubis!*

"Well, well, well," he said, leering at me with an evil smile that showed off two rows of razor-sharp teeth. "We meet again, Wildcat. And without all your little friends. Pity."

He held up the skeleton key he'd just used to lock me in.

I growled and clawed at him through the bars, but he backed away, his long nails scraping against the stone floor.

He was out of reach. *If only I could reach him, I would . . . I would . . . Probably get killed.* I let out a roar full of anger and despair.

He laughed, as if my rage were music to his ears. "Now, now," he said. "No need for that. You're trapped now, you see. I'm so glad you were able to find my temple, though I daresay you had some help from friends of mine who steered you in the right direction."

I thought of the dogs, the birds, the girl who'd stood beside me in front of Shiva. *They were all in on it.* Had my seeing the newspaper article about the artifact being found at the temple even been an accident? Maybe Kiah had laid it out for me to find, knowing it would lead me here.

"Centuries ago," Anubis continued, "the lion Wildcat helped lock the Hindu god Shiva inside the statue you saw upstairs. It was a wrong that I will soon make right. At midnight I shall bring Shiva back to life to take his rightful place among the Brotherhood of Chaos! And you, my captive lion"—he reached one long clawed finger between the wires of the cage and scraped his disgusting black nail down my face—"you will help me make it happen."

chapter 13
Ana

WHEN THE PLANE TOUCHED DOWN AT A SMALL PRIVATE airport in Mumbai that night, the tingling in my spine returned with a vengeance. It had taken a whole day to fly there from Cancún, so it was a relief to feel Shani's presence. *We're coming, Shani,* I thought, hoping she could hear me.

Antonio maneuvered into a hanger barely bigger than the plane and came to a stop.

"Please tell me we're here," Lin said. "This tingling in my spine is driving me nuts. The sooner we find Shani, the better."

"Seriously," Doli added. "Next time one of you sister cats needs me, just pick up a phone and call."

"Look, I know this magical connection stuff is annoying," I replied, looking at the night sky through the small oval window, "but as long as we feel it, it must mean Shani is alive. And if my instincts are right, we need to get to her right away."

After Antonio escorted us off the plane, he looked around

THE CIRCLE OF LIES

uncertainly, as if he were reluctant to let us go. "So you're going straight to Mr. Massri's house now, yes?"

"Yes, and Ms. Benitez said she'll be meeting us here as soon as she can," I said.

"You know, to help us with our, um, research project," Lin added.

Antonio quirked his lip, tilting his head and regarding us from the corner of his eyes. "Right, research project," he said, as if he knew exactly what we were up to. Ms. Benitez had been the one to call him and tell him to take us to Mumbai, so maybe he really did know. It wasn't easy figuring out who we could trust, but I had a strong feeling that Antonio was on our side. I hoped so, since I was leaving the vase along with our bags on the jet. We didn't know what we'd be facing, but it seemed best to travel light.

He handed us several bills that he said we should exchange for rupees before we left the airport. Then he wished us luck, reminded us that we had his cell phone number if we needed him, and got back on the plane. Once again we were on our own.

I picked up the cat and draped her over my shoulders, her rumbling purr vibrating against my neck. I looked at Doli and Lin, trying to muster my courage. "Let's go save our friend."

As soon as I opened the taxicab door and stepped out, the black cat took off running into the bushes.

Doli sighed. "That cat never sticks around to pay the cab fare. What a mooch!"

"Yeah, don't you hate that?" said Lin sarcastically, pulling out her wallet to pay the driver.

"Guys, would you quit joking around?" I said as we climbed out of the cab. "We've got to go get her. You know how many stray cats there must be in Mumbai? If she gets lost here, we'll never find her again."

"Pshh . . . Are you kidding?" Lin scoffed. "That cat knows how to take care of herself better than we do."

Doli flung her arm around my shoulder. "Lin's right. She always ends up exactly where she needs to be. And I think we all know by now that she's no ordinary— Whoa."

Doli was staring straight ahead, openmouthed, her neck craning up slowly. I followed her gaze, and my jaw fell open too.

Before us stood a towering glass apartment building with elegant curved balconies hugging the corners on each side. And a long dark green awning extended out over the sidewalk, giving the high-rise the look of a high-class Manhattan hotel.

"I knew her dad was a diplomat, but this place is amazing," I gushed.

"Eh, it's all right," Lin said, shrugging it off. "A little flashy for my taste." Doli and I shared a look. I guessed we had to cut her some slack. Lin had come a long way from the spoiled princess I had first met when I'd gotten to Temple. But we knew she was still struggling with the fact that her family had lost most of their money and she was now closer to being one of the "poor people" she used to look down on.

Like the movie star's daughter she was, Lin sauntered past the doorman as if she owned the place, and he didn't stop her.

Soon we were outside apartment 14H, knocking on the door. After a minute the door swung open, and we were faced with a tall man with graying hair at his temples and large brown eyes that looked just like Shani's. The aroma of cilantro and basil wafted into the hall.

"Yes?" he said, staring at us curiously. I'm sure it wasn't every day that three random teenagers just showed up on his doorstep.

"Are you Mr. Massri?" I asked.

"I am. How can I help you?"

Doli tried to peek into the apartment. "Are we interrupting your dinner?"

"Yes, actually," Mr. Massri said, shifting to block her view. "And I'd like to get back to it. So can you kindly tell me what it is you want?"

"We need to see your daughter, sir," Lin said.

Mr. Massri nodded and called over his shoulder, "Sweetie? I think some of your school friends are here to see you. Please make it fast."

He moved aside, and a slim Indian girl around our age stepped into the doorway. I didn't know who she was, but she wasn't Shani—and she didn't look happy to see us at all. "Shani's friends," she hissed. "What are *you* doing here? You aren't welcome."

I blinked in surprise. Hadn't Shani told us her sisters were off at university and boarding school? And if this was her sister, how come she knew who we were but her father didn't? Worst of all, why were we *unwelcome*?

A tiny part of me wondered whether it was because of what had happened with Principal Ferris. Maybe Shani really didn't want us here. But I shook the thought from my head. In my gut I knew our friend needed us, and until I saw her with my own eyes, I wouldn't move a muscle.

"We want to see Shani," I repeated.

"Who cares what you want? We're trying to eat dinner. You need to go."

Lin crossed her arms and planted her feet. "We're not going anywhere until we see her."

"I said get lost!" the girl hissed.

"Kiah," Mr. Massri said, approaching the door again. If he noticed the tension in the air, he gave no outward sign. He simply looked at the girl and nodded toward the kitchen. "Your dinner is getting cold. Your friends need to go now."

Shani doesn't have a sister named Kiah, does she? I glanced curiously at my friends, and though I knew they couldn't read my thoughts in our human guises, they looked just as confused as I felt.

"They're no friends of mine," Kiah said. "I don't know why they're bothering us. I think they're selling something."

By the look on Mr. Massri's face, I could see our window of opportunity shrinking. Soon this door would slam in our faces.

"Mr. Massri!" I shouted, thinking desperately. "Can I . . . use your bathroom? Please? It's an emergency." I started squirming and dancing where I stood. He pressed his lips together, clearly debating what to do. *"Please,"* I begged. "I'm not feeling well."

Finally, still looking very confused, he opened the door wider. Kiah glared at him. "Fine," he said. "It's down the hall and to the left. But after that you and your friends had better go. We're not interested in buying whatever you're here to sell."

I nodded enthusiastically. "Okay, you've got it." As I hustled past Doli and Lin, I whispered, "If I'm not out in ten minutes, call the police."

I ran for the bathroom and closed the door. After a couple of minutes I eased the door open, listening to make sure that Mr. Massri and Kiah had gone back to the dining room on the other side of the apartment. When I heard the chatter and clinking silverware of the family eating dinner, I crept down the hall in the opposite direction from the living room and started peeking in doors.

The first bedroom clearly belonged to Shani's father. There was a large king-size bed in the middle of the room and a dark wood dresser against the wall. On top of the dresser were framed photographs. One was of Mr. Massri and a tall beautiful woman in a red wedding sari. Next to it was a picture of Kiah in her school uniform. Still another was of all three of them together, standing in front of a temple. There were framed photos on the walls, too.

Shani's missing from all of them, I realized.

I tiptoed out of there and snuck into another room farther down the hall. This one had walls plastered with pictures of Kiah and what I assumed were her friends and of random celebrities. But there were two twin beds in the room, and one of them had been stripped bare.

I opened the closet to see if Shani's clothes were there, but nothing on the hangers looked like hers. Even her suitcase was missing. In fact, not one item in the room belonged to Shani. It was as if she had never been there at all. But that couldn't be. If she had never made it to her father's apartment, wouldn't she have said so that first night when she'd texted to tell us she missed us? Wait a minute. . . . When I'd told Mr. Massri we were here to see his daughter, he never asked, *Which one?*

Every mental alarm I had went off in that moment.

I ran full speed back down the hall and into the dining room, where Mr. Massri, Kiah, and the beautiful woman I'd seen in the photographs were sitting around a long dining room table. "Mr. Massri, where is your daughter *Shani*?" I blurted.

Mr. Massri put his fork down and gave me a blank look. "I don't *have* a daughter named Shani," he said. "Kiah is the only daughter I have."

My breath came up short. "What?"

Kiah got out of her chair and gave me a withering look. "Are you deaf? He said I'm his only daughter, not that it's any of your business." She took two quick strides over to me, grabbed my arm, and squeezed it painfully as she pulled me toward the door. Just before she opened it, she got right in my face and said, "You're officially trespassing. If I catch you here again, I won't be as nice."

Even if she hadn't been hurting my arm, and even if she hadn't been the rudest person I'd met since Nicole, Kiah would have rubbed me the wrong way. Just being near her made all the hairs on my arms stand up, and her breath—the smell was faint, but I recognized a hint of something rotten.

She whipped open the door and shoved me into the hallway, sending me barreling into a surprised Lin's arms.

"And stay out!" she cried.

Doli looked at me with wide eyes. "Was Shani in there?"

I shook my head. "No. I think something's happened to her, and Kiah here knows what it is."

Kiah was still standing in the doorway, glaring at us. Lin looked at her and narrowed her eyes. "What have you done to her?"

Kiah snorted. "The question is, what could I do to *you*?"

She started to slam the door, just as I'd suspected she would, but Lin stuck her foot out to keep the door open. "We're going to find Shani, whether you like it or not. And then we're coming back here for you!"

Kiah lifted her foot as if she were about to stomp on Lin's, so I pulled Lin back, and the door snapped shut.

And as we stood there staring at the golden 14H on the outside of the door, we heard a long, low growl from inside the apartment—one that no human could make.

chapter 14
Shani

I CAN'T TRANSFORM, I CAN'T TRANSFORM! I SPUN IN TIGHT circles behind the bars. I was doing everything right—thinking human thoughts, picturing myself doing human things—but nothing, nothing would work. My hands remained paws, my teeth stayed long and sharp, and my cries for help all came out as roars.

Anubis stood watching me from outside the cage, laughing a gravelly, evil laugh. "Don't you understand?" he said. "Your struggling is useless. My magic is holding you in this form. For now, I need you to remain a Wildcat."

I glared at him. *Why?*

He gave me a tooth-filled smile. "Centuries ago it was the roar of a lion Wildcat that imprisoned Shiva in the statue. Now it is the roar of a lion Wildcat—yours—that will set him free!"

His eyes filled with a maniacal glee. *If only I could*

break through these bars . . . I snarled, thinking of all the possibilities.

"Besides, this way I don't have to hear you blather on and on. Truly, if I'd had to listen to one more of you Temple Academy girls prattle on about absolutely nothing, I'd have sent myself back to the underworld for good. I've done you a favor by preventing your return to human form.

"But don't worry, I won't keep you prisoner forever. Once you have served your purpose, I will take your life and set *you* free as well. In one stroke I will gain a powerful ally and be rid of one pesky Wildcat!" He lifted his snout to the ceiling then as he let out a loud, horrifying laugh.

I growled, wishing he could hear all my murderous thoughts, but the longer I growled, the more satisfied he looked.

"Aww . . . tsk, tsk, tsk . . . Did you actually believe Ixchel when she told you that you could defeat me? Foolish girl. Every day I get closer to waking the Brotherhood, and soon I will be ready to show the world my power and take over the earth. I have already brought Quetzalcoatl back into the mortal realm. Only a few more additions, and I will have all I need to complete my plan!"

I stopped my restless pacing. *Do the Wildcats know about that?* If they did, they hadn't mentioned it in any of their texts or e-mails. At least, they hadn't said anything up to the time when Dad confiscated my phone and took the Internet away. I hoped by now that my friends had phoned Ms. Benitez and they were all over this Quetzal-whatchamacallit. But it was just as likely that they were completely in the dark, and the only person who could warn them was stuck in this stupid cage.

RRRROWWWRRR! I roared again, as ferociously as I could. If I couldn't tear him to shreds, I could at least scare the stuffing out of him. But Anubis didn't even flinch. Instead he rocked back on his clawed feet and laughed. When he stopped, he lowered his voice and spoke. Somehow, his quiet voice was far more frightening than my deafening roar.

"You do *not* threaten me, child. You may be endowed with ancient power, but you clearly lack intelligence. You've seen how easy it was to lure you to my temple, just as my minion Nicole was able to lure you to the gym that fateful night. All she had to do was pretend to be Ana's aunt, and, like the predictable children you are, you came running. I had hoped that all four of you would be expelled and separated, but no matter. It was you who mattered the most."

Anubis spun around. When he turned back to me, he'd transformed into the smiling Dr. Logan with his linen suit and straight white teeth. "Then that heartbroken fool of a principal kicked you out, just as I knew she would, and your mother sent you packing to India, delivering you into my clutches, right on schedule."

I glared at him, seething with hatred. He'd orchestrated everything! That meant he knew all about my parents' divorce, my school record. He'd been watching me, researching me, pulling invisible strings I hadn't even known were there.

Dr. Logan tsked at me. "Come now, Shani. There's no reason to be upset. The Brotherhood will expand and be much more powerful than it has been in centuries, and I owe it all to you."

I saw red. I lunged at Dr. Logan, but all I managed to do was bang painfully into the metal bars of the cage.

"See what I mean?" said Anubis, transforming back to his hideous jackal form. "You're not too bright. I've already told you: You're trapped, and there's nothing you or any of your friends can do about it now."

With a sinking feeling I realized he had every reason to gloat. I'd walked right into his trap like a moth flying into an electric bug zapper. Even worse, I hadn't told anyone that I was going to the temple—not my dad, not Sonia. And I hadn't e-mailed Doli, Lin, or Ana either. I had reached out with my mind, but I doubted they could hear me.

No one is coming to save me, I thought with miserable clarity. *I'm going down, and whether I want to or not, I'm taking the whole world with me.*

chapter 15
Ana

"So that went well." Doli stared up at Shani's shining glass apartment building.

"Totally," Lin said sarcastically. "We didn't find Shani, Ana almost got her arm ripped off, and we have no idea what to do next. Complete success."

"Guys," I said, still rubbing my arm where Kiah's grip had left five angry red indents. "That wasn't our best moment, but it wasn't a total fail. Ms. Benitez was right. There is something seriously weird going on here." I told them about the odd lack of Shani inside the apartment, and how her father didn't seem to remember her at all. "At least now we know that Shani really *does* need our help. We just have to decide what to do."

Lin looked around at the darkening sky, which cast shadows onto the unfamiliar streets around us. "I say we find the cat, then go back to the jet and regroup," she advised. "It's getting late, and I'm not feeling too safe out here on our own. Plus, we don't have anywhere to sleep."

Doli shook her head vehemently. "If Shani's really in trouble, every second counts. Going all the way back to the airport would take too long. Kiah is obviously hiding what she knows. There's got to be something we can do right here."

"I think if we go back inside, the doorman won't be so friendly," I said. "I'm pretty sure Kiah will have called downstairs and told him not to let us back in."

All of us were silent for a minute, scrambling for ideas. Finally, Lin smiled at me and said, "WWSD?"

"You have an idea?" I said hopefully.

"If Shani were here, she'd find some techie way to find one of us, right? So why don't we do the same thing to find her? Even if she hasn't been able to use it for some reason, Shani would never go anywhere without her cell phone. Doesn't hers have one of those tracking things in it so you can find it in case you lose it?"

"That's brilliant, Lin!" I cried. "The only thing is, to get that info you have to either be the owner of the phone or a parent. None of us sound very parental."

Doli smiled. "If Shani were here, she'd just hack into the phone company's GPS system and get the information herself."

"Figures," I said, lifting my arms and letting them flap back against the sides of my legs. "The one person who could help us find Shani is Shani."

Lin fished in her pocket and pulled out her smartphone. "Let me try calling Antonio," Lin said. "Maybe he'll know how to get the information we need."

Doli raised her eyebrows. "Do you have an international plan, Lin? Because otherwise . . ."

Lin snorted. "Do I have an international plan? Does the daughter of a diplomat and an A-list Chinese actress have an international plan? I don't know, let's see . . ." She started pressing buttons and scrolling through her contacts—

GROWWWWLLLLL!

Startled by the loud noise behind us, I turned to see three mangy-looking dogs approaching with their tails stiff and pointed in the air.

"We have company!" I yelled, nudging Lin and Doli, who both turned around, and Lin screamed in surprise. The three of us pressed together, each of us trying simultaneously to hide behind our friends and protect them.

Drool streamed from the dogs' open jaws, and their shoulder blades stuck up in sharp angles as they inched forward. The dog in front, who I took to be the pack leader, had an extra long snout and bristly ears, and maybe I was just imaging things, but those eyes—they reminded me of Kiah. *Could it be . . .*

"We've got to transform," Lin said. "Or they're going to have us for dinner."

I looked left and right. The street was full of pedestrians

walking around, going about their day. These dogs would be no match for us as big cats, but if we transformed here, we'd be seen and would probably cause a stampede. "We can't do that," I said. "Not out in the open. Let's back up, nice and slow. Maybe they'll leave us alone."

We each took a few halting steps backward, watching the dogs carefully. Suddenly one of them lunged, backing us all the way against the side of a nearby storefront. Some of the passersby glanced our way, but no one stopped to help. Maybe the roving band of stray dogs was a common sight around here, but my heart was beating out of control.

"What do we do?" Doli yelled.

I thought quickly. "We split up, and *run!*" I shoved Doli to the left and Lin to my right. Then I ducked down the side street behind me, a narrow one-way road with only two working streetlights. Just as I'd hoped, the dogs split up too. I could hear the nails of the other two dogs scraping against the pavement as they took off after Doli and Lin. I could feel the dog behind me gaining ground, but I dodged into a shadowy alcove. It was the perfect place to shift.

Almost instantly I felt my skin dissolve into golden spotted fur, and my whiskers twitched in the breeze. I ran, my strides lengthening with every step. Even though I could take the dog in this form, I would avoid a fight if I could. Once, when I was younger, I had asked Uncle Mec what to do if kids bullied me at school. *Corre si puedes, pelea si debes,* he had said. Run if you can, fight if you must. I hoped that this time, running would be enough.

I could no longer hear the dog following me. It must have seen me change and slowed down, probably wondering if it was worth it to keep up the pursuit. Still, I wanted to put more distance between us. At the end of the alley I saw a low wall that would give me the perfect step up onto the roof of the building.

I scaled the wall easily and climbed onto the roof. I looked down, and in addition to the dog, I was stunned to see the black cat. *There she is!* I thought.

I saw the dog reach the wall and stop short. It raised up onto its hind legs and pawed at the surface. It couldn't make the jump. The black cat looked at the dog with disdain and hissed. The dog whimpered and backed off, retreating down the alley, but the cat stayed put, as if to stand guard. I kept going, confident she would find me later. Now that I had a moment to think without being chased, I lifted my nose to the air to see if I could smell Doli and Lin, but instead I caught a hint of something familiar—henna ink, toasted almonds, and worn-in sneakers. *Shani!* She'd come this way! Even if she wasn't here now, she had been at some point.

Lin, Doli—are you okay?

Yes. I ditched the leader, Lin's answer echoed in my mind. *Embarrassingly easy to do.*

Mine got scared and ran away, Doli said. *Didn't want to tangle with a puma.*

Good. I smell Shani! Try to follow her scent.

On it, Doli responded.

Me too, Lin said.

I inhaled deeply, letting my whiskers feel for subtle changes in the wind. But there were so many different new scents here, many of them belonging to animals. I couldn't pick one out from another. They pressed in from all sides—roasting chickens, perfume, Darjeeling tea, cinnamon and red chili, pigeons and Persian cats, salt water and sweat . . . How was I supposed to find Shani's scent in all this?

Above me a woman opened her window to shake out a dusty rug. She glanced down and saw me, and her eyes widened in alarm. She slammed the window shut. I moved on. By the time she peeked out again to confirm what she'd seen, I would be gone and she would think I had just been a trick of the light.

I suddenly heard a familiar roar in the distance. *Lin!* I took off across rooftops, following the sound. A few blocks away I saw the golden spires of a temple rising into the sky, and an orange flag flapping in the wind. I found a way back down to street level and did my best to stay in the shadows. I lifted my nose again to sniff at the air, and this time the smell of almonds and Shani's sneakers was unmistakable.

As I came to the end of the marketplace across from the temple, I spotted one of the dogs that had tried to attack us. It was the pack leader, the one I thought reminded me of Kiah.

The dog was pacing back and forth outside the entrance, twisting its head in every direction. This must have been the dog that had been chasing Lin and lost her. I watched as the dog slowly lowered its tail and licked its mouth. It was giving up, I realized. It scratched furiously behind one ear, then ducked into the narrow alley to the side of the temple.

A few seconds later Kiah walked out of the same alley, brushing off a maroon-and-white school uniform and combing her hair into place with her hands.

I knew it! Kiah was a shape-shifter like Nicole, but instead of a hyena, she was a feral dog. A soft growl from behind me drew my attention away from her. A tiger was approaching, panting quietly, and just behind was a regal-looking puma, nearly invisible in the dark, except for her luminous yellow eyes. Lin chuffed and padded off toward the entrance of a nearby park that looked like it had been closed for the night. We passed by the locked gate and jumped easily over the stone walls that stretched out on either side of the entrance.

As soon as we were safely inside the park and were sure no one could see us, we transformed.

"Shani is in the temple," Lin said immediately, still trying to catch her breath. "I'm sure of it."

"I smelled her in there too," Doli said.

"Me too. Guess we don't need to find her phone after all," I said.

We heard a rustling in a bush near the wall, and out strode

the black cat, her emerald eyes glowing like headlights in the dark. She rubbed up against each of our legs, then walked back to the locked gate and slithered underneath it through the gap at the bottom. She took a few steps toward the temple and looked back at us as if to say, *What are you waiting for?*

I laughed. "I guess it's unanimous."

Since we couldn't go the same way the cat had, we carefully climbed over the wall and jumped down on the other side. We started toward the temple, but Lin shot her hand out and grabbed my shoulder. "Those dogs might be watching the temple," she said. "Maybe we shouldn't approach so out in the open."

I looked around warily. "Yeah, you're right. Let's cut through the market. It's right across the street from the entrance."

Doli looked conflicted, clearly itching to just go straight to the temple, but in the end she relented. "Fine. Let's just make it fast."

Soon we were pushing through the crowds of Dadar Phool Gali, passing by cloth-lined bins filled with cardamom seeds and sweet orange curry, baskets of pink roses and yellow chrysanthemums, and stands of fresh green vegetables.

But suddenly someone bumped right into me, too hard to be an accident, even in this crowded market. The bump pushed me into Doli and Lin, who both shouted "Hey!" and glared at me.

I wheeled around to see who had pushed me. "What are you—" I started. But I trailed off when I realized I was facing a small elderly man with eyes that crinkled in the corners. He was holding three copper cups.

"Forgive me," he said. He forced one cup into each of our hands.

"Who *is* this guy?" Doli asked.

I shook my head at her. "I don't know." Then I turned back to the man. "What is this?" I asked, confused.

He gestured that I should lift the cup and drink.

"Sorry, my mother always told me not to drink anything given to me by a total stranger," Lin protested, trying to hand the cup back.

But the man shook his head and smiled. He curved his fingers into a *C*, and with his thumb against his bottom lip, tilted his hand up as if to say, *Drink, drink.*

I leaned my face over the cup, taking in the scent of rich vanilla chai. It smelled heavenly. "I'll drink it first," I offered, "and I'll tell you if it's okay."

"No offense, Ana," Lin said, "but that's kind of a dumb plan. If it's not okay, you won't taste anything; you'll just drop dead."

I knew she was right, yet something about the man's kind face told me I could trust him. "I'm going with my gut," I said.

Doli still eyed the man with a measure of suspicion. "All right. If anything happens, though, I'm calling the police on this guy."

"Fair enough." I closed my eyes and drank the whole cup down, feeling its warmth spread through my chest. But it was more than just warmth. As soon as the delicious tea touched my lips and slid down my throat, I knew I'd never tasted anything quite like it. As the vanilla flavor burst onto my tongue, a strange tingle spread through my body, making me feel stronger and more alive. When I opened my eyes again, colors seemed a little brighter, and I was filled with a sense of confidence—like nothing could hurt me. The last time I'd felt that way had been when we had touched the magical orb that had released our Wildcat powers. "Mmm . . . ," I said, looking at the man in astonishment.

"So it's good?" Lin asked.

"No," I said, never taking my eyes from the tea seller. "It's awesome."

The other girls drank the tea in their cups too and were just as happy that they had. Lin reached into her pocket and pulled out a few rupees to hand to the old man, but he held his hand up, refusing the coins. Instead he handed each of us a small bouquet of flowers tied with an orange satin ribbon, and pointed to the temple. "Offering for Ganesh," he said.

He knows we're heading to the temple, I thought. *How?*

It was just one more unanswered question. I knew we had to get going. I bowed to him and said, "We thank you." Lin and Doli did the same, and he gave us appreciative nods. I walked out of the market feeling braver and warmer but still afraid.

As we headed toward the temple, which seemed to almost

glow against the burning sunset, the black cat took off into an alley beside it.

"There she goes again," Doli commented. "Getting out of harm's way. Hope she doesn't know something we don't."

I hoped not too. But I couldn't help but wonder: *What are we walking into?*

chapter 16
Shani

I WOKE UP IN MY CAGE, FEELING COMPLETELY DRAINED. When had I fallen asleep? I didn't know. The last thing I remembered was staring at Anubis's evil face, wanting to tear it off, and then nothing. I looked around and found him sitting on the wooden throne atop the altar of human bones. *Doesn't he ever sleep?* Maybe as a god of the underworld, he was beyond sleep. Even now he was leering at me in a way that made my skin crawl.

Or it *would* have made my skin crawl, if I weren't still covered in my feline fur. I had never stayed in my lion form this long, and now I knew why. It was exhausting! There seemed to be a time limit on how long I could be in a magical state of being, and I had passed it hours ago. I slowly got to my feet, feeling shaky and weak. Even if Anubis opened my cage right now, I didn't think I'd have the strength to fight him.

I guessed I had to accept it. There was no way out. No

clever hacking tricks were going to save me this time. Even being a kick-butt magical lion was a liability right now. Seemed as good a time as any to have a little heart-to-heart with myself.

Voice of Reason: So, Shani, looks like you've gotten yourself into a fine mess, huh?

Me: Gee, really? Thanks for pointing that out, Captain Obvious. I hadn't noticed.

Voice of Reason: Hey, no need to shoot the messenger. It's your own fault you're in this cage.

Me: What? How do you figure that?

Voice of Reason: Think hard, and don't get defensive. Is there any way you could have avoided ending up in a dungeon, about to help the god of the underworld destroy the planet?

Me: Hmmm . . .

Voice of Reason: Take your time. I'll wait.

Me: Well, I guess I could have ignored that article in the paper and not come on my own to what I had a hunch was a dangerous place.

Voice of Reason: Good! Excellent start. Anything else? Think back a little further.

Me: You mean what I did at the gym? But I saved everybody!

Voice of Reason: True. But you were only able to do that because . . .

Me: (hanging my head) I hacked into my principal's account and stole her password.

Voice of Reason: There you go. And before that . . .

Me: Coach Lawson?

Voice of Reason: Are you asking or telling me?

Me: (sigh) Coach Lawson.

Voice of Reason: You're making excellent progress. Really great. But maybe we should go back even further. Back to where all this trouble began.

Me: (long silence) Ms. Benitez. I accepted her invitation to the museum that night. The night I became a Wildcat.

Voice of Reason: Even I have to admit, before that evening you were more or less a normal kid getting in a normal amount of trouble. And now, well . . .

Me: Right. Alone in a dungeon, about to help destroy the world.

Voice of Reason: I think we're done here.

I groaned. Had the best, most exciting thing to ever happen to me also been my worst mistake? Maybe so. And that's coming from a girl who's made plenty of mistakes. My inner voice was right. Before I had accepted that invitation to Ms. Benitez's reception in the museum that night—the night I'd met Ana and touched the globe that had activated my powers—I had been fine. Normal. Just another kid at a fancy-pants boarding school, keeping my hacking tricks under the radar and staying out of trouble.

Everything could have stayed that way too. But no, I had to go become friends with Doli, Ana, Lin, and Ms. Benitez— and look where that had gotten me. I owed some of my best memories of school to them. I had even done better in my classes. But I'd also been turned into some kind of avenging lion who was constantly being attacked by gods and demons.

Mom would just love this. She had always warned me about befriending other future criminal masterminds, but she'd never said a word about shape-shifting do-gooders out to save the world. I could almost see her shaking her head and saying, *You always pick the wrong friends.* I would have laughed if it hadn't been at least a little bit true. I guessed it didn't matter now. I would never see them again anyway. I sighed and slumped to the floor.

"Guys, over here! There's another room back here!"

My ears suddenly perked up. The voice was yelling from right above me.

"Is she in there?"

"I don't know."

"Lin, you just plowed that guy over!"

"Sorry."

I shot back up to my feet, my heart pounding. *I know those voices!* From the way Anubis stood up and scowled, I could tell he recognized them too. *My friends!* I didn't know how they'd found me, but I had never been so grateful. *I'm down here!* I yelled, but of course it came out as a cage-rattling roar.

They probably couldn't hear it anyway over the earsplitting banging of metal against metal. I realized they must have been trying to bust through the padlock on the metal gate separating the main room from the alcove that held the statue of Shiva.

"Shani! Are you down there?"

Yes! I thought as loudly as I could.

I heard a man's voice say something to them, probably telling them to keep their voices down and stop attacking the gate. Then Lin's voice: "If you don't want to be kitty chow, you'll get out of here right now!" I heard a deep growl, then the sound of someone screaming and footsteps running away.

Forget everything I said before, I thought. *My friends are awesome!*

"We don't have time for this," Lin said. "Let's just turn into Wildcats and knock the dang thing down."

"No, we can't," Ana pleaded. "We're in a temple full of people and—" She was cut off by the sound of a puma's roar, which sounded almost like the scream of an electric guitar.

"Too late," Lin said. Then she roared too. Soon Doli's and Lin's roars were joined by a third. I heard the metallic gate squeak and rattle once, twice, three times, then *snap!* It clattered against the stone floor. They must have found the hole I'd escaped through before, because a few seconds later the Wildcats leaped down the stairs one by one.

The first one down, Lin looked around at the engravings on the walls and thought, *What the . . .*

Doli and Ana followed right behind and gasped when they saw the images of suffering littering the walls.

It's another Brotherhood of Chaos temple, Ana thought. *What do we do now?*

You can start by getting me out of here! I urged, and even the voice in my head sounded simultaneously overjoyed and worn out.

All three Wildcats turned in my direction, and their eyes grew wide.

Shani! What happened to you? Doli cried, running over to the cage.

Anubis lured me down here and then threw me into this cage. He needs my roar to release another god. Watch out. He's right over— I broke off. When I looked over at the throne of bones, I saw that Anubis was gone. But how? As far as I could see, there was only one way out. *He was right there,* I said feebly.

Forget about him for now, Doli said. *Let's get you out of there.* She reared up on her hind legs and clawed at the lock, but it didn't budge. Her eyes shifted to the thick wires forming the bars on the cage. *Back up, Shani.*

Realizing what she was going to do, I shook my head. *No, don't. You'll get hurt. Your jaws aren't strong enough. . . .*

Doli huffed. *Of course they are. How do you think pumas in the wild are able to take down prey twice their size?* With that, she opened her jaws wide and attacked the cage as if it were Anubis himself. She clamped down on the wires and tugged at them with all her might, using her long tail for balance. I heard the ping and twang of wires snapping as she tore into them with her powerful teeth. Then, with one final yank, Doli ripped a gaping hole in the gate. The tension of the enclosure broken, all the wires unraveled and fell away. Doli spit out what looked like metal worms. The white fur around her mouth was covered in blood.

I leaped out of the cage and rubbed my head against Doli's. *Thank you! I'll never doubt you again, boss lady!*

Better not.

Now that you're free, any idea where Anubis ran off to? Ana asked.

Maybe he saw us and just gave up and went back to the underworld? Doli said hopefully.

Doubt it, I said. *Anubis had some pretty big plans for me.* I filled them in on the statue of Shiva and how Anubis planned to use my roar to bring him back to life. *Everything that happened back at Temple—the fake call from Ana's aunt, me getting kicked out of school—it was all part of his plan to get me here.*

Diabolical! Lin said. *Anybody who would go through that much trouble isn't going to let us just walk out of here.*

As if on cue, an eagle suddenly soared out of nowhere and swooped down on us with a terrible scream.

Aw, not this again, I said. Before the bird had a chance to fly past us, I pounced and sank my claws into one of its wings, bringing it down. It tried to claw at me, but I bent my head and ripped into its throat. One good thing—really, the *only* good thing—about getting ambushed by eagles earlier when I'd been all by myself was that it had made me kind of a pro at killing them. Now that I had learned how to time my attack and come in at just the right angle, taking them down was easy.

Whoa, Ana said. *Got a few anger-management issues?*

When it comes to those birds, absolutely.

Well, that's good, because here come some more.

Just as they had upstairs, the eagle Chaos Spirits started multiplying. One became two then became six. . . . It was hard to see how they were even doing it. This time there were no Eddie the Eagle banners or Temple T-shirts to help them. They just kept dividing, like in that video we'd watched in biology class about bacteria cells splitting in half to reproduce. I must have fallen asleep during the part when cells divided and became a legion of soul-crushing demons.

Soon the room filled up with flapping brown wings that together sounded like water rushing over the edge of a cliff and crashing into the rocks below. My heart banged in my chest. I could actually feel a breeze as the motion of their wings stirred the stagnant air of the basement temple, the foul odor of death growing stronger in my nose. But at least I wasn't alone, I reminded myself. I had three Wildcats by my side, and that was all I needed.

It's time for payback! I charged into the flock of birds, my claws slashing as I went. The eagles flapped their massive wings in Lin's face, knocking her to the ground, but she quickly regrouped, grabbing up the broken wires in her mouth and flinging them at the birds. A frayed edge pierced one of the birds in its chest, sending it reeling to the floor, and Ana finished it off with one powerful chomp.

In answer, three eagles attacked at once, sinking their talons deep into Ana's leg and pecking bloody welts into her thigh. She roared, rolling over and crushing them under her weight. Nice! I'd have to remember that move. Still, for every eagle we brought down, three more showed up, and all of us were already bleeding from patches where tufts of fur had been ripped out.

We have to get out of here! Ana yelled.

But we couldn't. At the foot of the stairs perched four of the largest eagles I'd ever seen, blocking the only exit. It must have been their job to make sure we couldn't run away.

I looked around, thinking furiously. There was no water here like in the gym . . . but there *was* fire. I looked at the throne where Anubis had sat watching me. It was almost the only thing in the temple that wasn't made of bones. The throne itself was made of dark wood—flammable dark wood. I reached deep into myself and dredged up the last drops of energy I could find. *Ana, help me!*

I led the way over to the throne and crouched behind it.

Ana joined me. *Smash it,* I said. *We need kindling.* Catching on right away, Ana placed her strong paws on the back the chair. Together we rocked it back and forth until it tumbled from its perch and splintered apart, breaking into several pieces.

We pulled the pieces to a space near one of the torches on the wall. I jumped up and knocked the torch out of place. It landed right in the middle of the remains of the throne. The blaze grew fast, licking at the walls. We ran back to the cage, where Lin and Doli were still fighting. The eagles had gained the upper hand—upper *wing?*—and immediately talons aimed for our faces. I closed my eyes and batted them away. *The best defense is a good offense,* I thought. I leaped forward and galloped through the crowd of birds. Finally a few of them winged back to avoid the crush of my teeth—and flew right into the flames. Those few were all I needed.

When they felt the fire catch on their wings, they panicked and flew into the thick of the other birds, trying to beat out the flames. But all it did was spread the fire. In minutes, eagles were screeching in pain and the fire was spreading, smoke and the smell of singed feathers filling the underground chamber.

Now! Let's go! I yelled. We clambered over the bones covering the floor and found the steps. We ran up the stairs to the small room with the statue of Shiva, but we stopped short when we reached the top. A man sat in front of the statue. His head was bowed, and his hands were palms-up on his folded legs, his middle fingers touching the tips of his thumbs. We all exchanged puzzled looks.

Is he a tourist? I asked.

Looks like he's meditating, but if he doesn't get out of here, he's going to get himself killed, Doli stated matter-of-factly.

I crept closer, trying to get a better look. When I bent my neck and caught a glimpse of the man's peaceful smile and closed eyes, I jumped in shock, my tale swishing. *It's the tea seller from the market!*

Ana, do you think he followed us here? Doli wondered.

I don't know, she said. *But he was kind to us. We can't just leave him. He's in danger here.*

Then let's scare him so bad, he'll go screaming like that guard did. Lin got right in the old man's face and let out a terrifying growl. But the man didn't move a muscle.

Maybe he's deaf, Ana guessed. *He won't move.*

Doli shook her head. *Or maybe he's in some really deep meditation. Hey, let's put the broken gate over the hole in the floor. It'll slow down any surviving eagles or . . .*

She started toward the broken remnants of the gate, all of us following behind, but she stopped dead in her tracks. The twisted scraps of metal had suddenly sprung from the floor, straightening and snapping back into position, reforming into the gate before our eyes. I heard Lin roar in frustration, but the sound only seemed to bounce off the gate and echo meekly back, like the metal had absorbed the brunt of its volume. *No one will be able to hear us roar, no one will be able to hear us scream,* I thought.

Then Anubis materialized out of thin air, glaring at us from in front of the soundproof gate. That was freaky enough. Even scarier, he looked just past us, and his face contorted in fear. We couldn't help it—we turned to see what was freaking out the Egyptian death god.

There, in front of the statue of Shiva, where the tea seller had been a second before, now sat a man with light blue skin and four arms.

I didn't know much about Hindu gods, but this one . . . I'd have bet my life on it. He was a god of protection. What was his name? It was on the tip of my tongue. . . .

Vishnu!

chapter 17

Ana

INSTEAD OF RAISING HIS STAFF AND SHOOTING OUT FIRE-works of magical energy, Anubis puffed up his chest and started chanting in some ancient language that practically dripped with evil. It jabbed into my ears like knives. I let out a whimper and dropped to the ground, desperately trying to cover my ears with my paws.

Vishnu started chanting too. If Anubis's words were knives, Vishnu's were a salve, soothing the pain. But Anubis raised his voice higher, and the poisonous words tumbled out faster, taking on the buzzing quality of a hive of angry wasps. When his chanting reached a fever pitch, he raised his staff and shot a bolt of energy—right at Doli! This time Ms. Benitez wasn't there to leap in the way and take the blast. The full force slammed into Doli's chest and knocked her to the ground. We opened our mouths and let out a chorus of bone-shaking roars. Too late, I realized that Shani had roared too.

Shani, no! I tried, but already Anubis had begun to laugh in triumph. Lin, Doli, and I had freed his prisoner, but he had still gotten the roar he wanted. I looked around with wild eyes as the chamber filled with an unnatural glow. The statue of Shiva was pulsing with a greenish-blue light, and its eyes slowly slid open. The statue was coming to life!

Shiva stretched his arm out, his palm facing us, and conjured a wall of light that sent us all flying across the room. The force pushed all the air out of my lungs, leaving me gasping for breath like a fish out of water. My chest burned, but I couldn't decide if the feeling came from the inside or out. We crashed to the floor near Doli, who had been knocked unconscious, our bones slamming painfully into the hard stone.

Lin groaned. *How are we supposed to fight that?*

I . . . I'm not sure we can, I answered. I felt my hope ebbing away.

Grinning down at us, Anubis called out, "Good-bye, Wildcats." He raised his staff and aimed it right at us. There was nowhere left to run. All we could do was pile in front of Doli to protect her as best we could and wait for our inevitable fate. The staff let out its stream of hot red light, but just before it reached us, it curved and bounced away from us—as if it had hit some invisible force field! I glanced over and saw that Vishnu was holding all four of his arms over us, creating a sky-blue dome of protection all around us.

I stared at Vishnu in amazement. *Why are you helping us?*

Like Ixchel, he could hear my thoughts, and he responded in kind, his voice seeming to come from all around me but also from inside me. *I am Vishnu,* he said, *the god of protection. I cannot help you in your fight, but I will do what I can to protect you.* As he spoke, two more blasts ricocheted off the dome and shot across the room, shattering a window.

"Stay out of this, Vishnu," Anubis barked. He changed the angle of his staff, aiming it directly at our only ally. The blast hit Vishnu's back, and for a moment the dome flickered and disappeared. Shiva took the opportunity to shoot searing bolts of magical heat at us. One of them grazed me and singed the hair on my neck. Another hit Shani square on the shoulder and burned the hair away, leaving a hot red scar, bubbling like boiling water. She roared, this time in pain. Quickly Vishnu recreated the dome and said, *Do not worry yourselves. The burn will heal.*

How do you know? I asked.

She, too, drank the tea. But its healing properties will not last forever.

The tea! That was why he had been so insistent that we drink it. He had known we were heading into a battle and would need a little extra protection. Maybe that meant Doli wouldn't end up in a coma like Ms. Benitez had. I looked around, trying to find a way out. But the newly restored gate blocked our escape back into the main room of the temple, and smoke rose in thick plumes from the hole in the floor.

Run if you can, fight if you must, Uncle Mec's voice sounded in my head. Well, there was nowhere to run, so that left only one option.

Anubis and Shiva were both good at using magic against us from far away, but how would they be close up? *Vishnu, can you cover us until we get right next to Anubis?*

Yes, but you must hurry.

Lin, let's go remind Anubis why he's afraid of us!

Right behind you, Ana.

Together we crept close to Anubis, protected by Vishnu's dome. Then at the last minute, I yelled, *Now, Vishnu!* and the protective veil fell back to cover only Shani and Doli. Lin and I each roared and swept out with our claws, hooking into Anubis's legs. He screamed in surprise and fell to his back. Without skipping a beat, Lin pounced on top of his chest while I slashed his legs. But before we could do anything else, Shiva shot a white-hot beam of light at us that sent us scrabbling back to the dome, ducking for cover.

Anubis got to his clawed feet and brushed himself, barely a scratch on him. Then he lifted his arms up in victory and shouted, "Your efforts are in vain. As you can see, Shiva's joining the brotherhood will change everything. He is the destroyer of worlds!" As if just hearing his name was his cue to destroy something, Shiva lifted his palm and shot out a pulse of light, and a huge section of the wall exploded into a heap of dust and rubble. "Destroying the world so we can remake it in our own evil image is exactly what the Brotherhood wants to do," Anubis went on. "It is a partnership made in hell!"

Then a new batch of eagles flew in through the shattered window, fresh and ready to fight. I counted about nine of them. Anubis turned his red-eyed glare on us. "Your time is up, Wildcats." He shot one devastating blast at Vishnu, who went flying and collapsed against the wall. The dome evaporated like steam.

The eagles descended, swooping by and gouging us with their talons as they passed. Blood—mine, I think—spattered across the floor. Shani tried to bat the evil birds, but her shoulder was not yet fully healed, and the motion made her wince in pain. Beside me, Doli's eyes fluttered open. *What's going on?* she asked, struggling to her feet.

We're getting our butts kicked, that's what, Shani replied.

Then let's retreat, Doli said sensibly.

There's nowhere to go! I cried. Even the windows the eagle spirits had entered through were too high for us to reach, Wildcat or no.

Doli looked around the room and nodded her head toward the hole in the floor. *There!* The small fire we'd set had turned into a raging inferno downstairs, and flames were now shooting up through the hole, licking at the ceiling of the chamber and creating a protective wall of fire. We'd been so focused on the battle at hand that we hadn't noticed. *The eagles won't go near the fire. And Anubis and Shiva won't be able to see us,* Doli said.

Good thinking. Let's go! I took off running and skidded to a stop behind the wall of flame. A bolt of angry white light collided with the fiery wall, and a burst of flame lashed out where the bolt had impacted. Soon all four of us were there, panting and licking at our wounds.

What are we going to do? Lin screamed. *We're outnumbered.*

She was right. We had to find a way to at least take the eagles out. But how? Nothing we had used to defeat them before would help us now. Here there were no water sprinklers, and the eagles had learned their lesson about fire. They wouldn't go near it again. Still, there weren't that many of them this time.

Why aren't they multiplying like they did before? I wondered.

Maybe the temple was the source of their power, Lin offered, *and now that that place is toast*—she nodded to the flames shooting out of the hole—*they can't multiply anymore.*

That means we have a chance! Shani cried. *What we need is a diversion. If one of us distracts Anubis and Shiva, the other three of us could take on the eagles and win.*

Okay, but who would be crazy enough to do that? It's beyond dangerous, Doli said.

I heard another bolt of energy hit the wall of fire, a harsh crackling sound that echoed around the chamber as the flames briefly flickered, before returning to full power. Shani looked into the fire, the red and orange flames reflected in her large eyes. *I'll do it,* she said.

What? No! You can't. Doli shook her head. *You've already sacrificed enough.*

Which means I have the least to lose, Shani said, her eyes glassy with tears.

I moved toward her. *No, Shani. You already got kicked out of school for protecting us.* I hung my head in shame. *I'm so sorry about that. I'm so sorry we didn't come forward and stand up for you.*

Shani shook her head at me. *No, don't apologize. What happened may not have been* all *my fault, but I was no innocent bystander.* I'm *the one who got myself kicked out of three boarding schools before I even got to Temple.* I'm *the one who refused to stop hacking—even when a good friend told me not to.* She glanced at Doli, who pawed at the ground. *Being part of the Hunters is the first time I've used my head to* help *people. If I don't make it, I'll feel good knowing I died doing the right thing.*

My eyes blurred with tears, but Lin stepped forward, so she was nose to nose with Shani, and said, *That's the dumbest thing I've ever heard! You actually think leaving us short another Hunter when we still have a bunch of Chaos Spirits to hunt would be helping us? And you think we're going to stand by and watch our friend go on a suicide mission alone? Did you completely lose your mind while you've been away? If that's what happens when we separate, maybe we should make a pact to never let that happen again. Obviously it scrambled your brains.*

Shani's eyes softened for a moment. As sarcastic as Lin was, we all knew what she was really saying was, *We love you.*

The crackling noises of the blasts' impacts were getting louder and more frequent, fireballs now bursting from the flames above our heads every few moments. Suddenly Shani's whole body seemed to fill with steely resolve. *There's no time for this,* she said. *Good luck, guys.*

She leaped over the flame in one smooth motion and ran straight for Anubis.

NO! I yelled. I leaped after her and lunged, and landed on her back, toppling her to the side.

Anubis smiled. "The Wildcats are fighting one another? Well, this is a pleasant surprise."

Get off me, Ana. What are you doing? Shani shouted.

This, I said. I got to my feet, and before Shani could stop me, I ran the rest of the way to Anubis. I felt almost as if I were running in slow motion. With every step, I thought about the fact that I still didn't know where Uncle Mec and Aunt Teppy were, and I was sure he did. Maybe he was even holding them hostage somewhere, like he had Shani. The anger that seeped into my chest at the thought of him hurting my family—the only family I had left—burned hotter than the flames consuming the underground temple. With a rage-filled growl, I sprang at him.

Anubis raised his arms, trying to protect his hideous face, but I clawed at his left arm, forcing it down. In his right he still held his staff, and he fumbled with it then, trying to aim it in my direction. I refused to let him get off that easily. I rose on my hind legs and clamped down on his elbow, sinking my fangs into his dark flesh. I instantly recoiled, tasting the bitterness of rot and death touch my tongue. And as I backed away, I saw that the arm I had bitten was unharmed. My jaws hadn't made a mark on him. Anubis followed my gaze and laughed, which only made me more furious. I charged again, this time leaping into the air, firing my full weight at his chest. He went down easily, his staff clattering to the ground. I climbed on top of him. Behind me I could hear the eagles' death cries as the other Wildcats brought them down. But I didn't look at them. I stared straight into Anubis's eyes. I wanted him to know who had defeated him before I grabbed his head in my jaws and ripped it right off.

But suddenly I heard the jingling of gold necklaces and the thud of heavy feet pounding their way toward me. I turned to see Shiva, standing upright and pulsing with bright green light. He raised his palm to me and said something in Hindi, and suddenly my vision exploded in a white-hot light. The next thing I knew, I was flying, helplessly sailing through the air. Time seemed to slow down. Below me I heard one of the Wildcats scream my name. Then the ground raced toward me—or I raced toward it—at a dizzying speed, and I landed with a crash. My vision exploded into white spots as pain twisted through me like burning barbed wire, and then I felt something on my right side break with an audible crunch.

Ana! Are you all right? Shani's panicked voice.

No, I thought—and everything went dark.

chapter 18
Shani

HERE'S SOMETHING I NEVER THOUGHT I'D HAVE TO SAY: AN eagle's feathers are hard to spit out after you tear their wings off. *Gross*, I thought, hacking up more feathers and pawing at my mouth. But at least the eagles themselves weren't as foul-tasting as the bats had been. Plus, I had to admit that sinking my teeth into their meaty flesh satisfied me in a way I couldn't quite explain. It was more than just the fact that I hadn't eaten much of anything in days. It was the hunter in me; some primal urge to dominate my prey had been fulfilled. I wondered if this was how my old cat used to feel whenever she killed a mouse and brought it to me as if it were a prize. As a vegetarian, I used to think that was disgusting, but now I understood.

When I lifted my head, I saw that Doli and Lin were finishing off the last two eagles that had dared attack us. Together we watched as ghostly shadows rose from the eagles' lifeless bodies and fled through the open window. I wished in vain that we had the vase with us to trap them inside, but I didn't know where Ana had left it.

That was when it dawned on me that I hadn't checked on Ana in a few minutes. I looked around and saw Shiva—just as he raised his hand and sent a burst of bright light at something. *A jaguar!* My heart leaped into my throat as the force of the attack sent her flying into the air.

Ana! I yowled, running to her side. I asked whether she was all right, but all I felt was the barest whisper of her voice in my mind, as if she were far, far away. *No.* Her eyes closed and the whisper faded into silence.

What happened? Doli asked, appearing with Lin on the other side of Ana.

I don't know. Shiva attacked her. I . . . don't think she's all right. She just—

Ahhh! A sudden pain in my back exploded like a firework and took my breath away. I turned my head to find Anubis's staff aimed right at me, red magical residue still shimmering in the air. He was shooting bolts of energy at me! Beside me Lin whined in pain and collapsed. Shiva smiled a peaceful smile that didn't make any sense and lowered his palm. He had attacked Lin, I realized, feeling sick to my stomach. Even without the eagles, we were no match for the two gods. Maybe if Ixchel were here, we'd have a fighting chance. But we were alone. *It's all over . . . ,* I thought. This temple was the last thing we would ever see.

Shiva raised his green hand again and turned to Doli, who cowered over Ana's body. The pulse of light ballooned out of his palm and arced through the air. But just inches away from Doli's closed eyes, the throbbing light split apart, running like several streams of water all around Doli, almost as if she had held up a shield. *How?*

I looked to see that Vishnu had recovered and was standing behind the fire, chanting something. *"Shree Gajanana, Jai Gajanana, Jai Jai Ganesh Morya,"* he repeated, over and over, words I recognized from the temple's sign of instructions near the entrance. The words filled me with hope and calm, but even while he continued chanting, his voice sounded in my mind. *I am weakened,* the voice said. *I cannot protect you for much longer. You must end this. . . .*

I turned to Lin and Doli. *We need to do something, now! Any ideas?*

Maybe we could jump out that window, Lin said, nodding weakly toward the broken window through which the Chaos Spirits had escaped.

We can't, Doli said. *Ana is still unconscious.* She nudged Ana's neck and got no response. *There are bound to be weapons somewhere in that temple downstairs. Maybe we can have Vishnu protect us from the fire long enough to get them.*

I shook my head. *We can't risk inviting more eagle spirits into this and getting trapped down there.*

Hurry, Vishnu urged us. *I can't hold on much longer.*

Lin's eyes suddenly brightened. *I got it. Remember what Anubis said about the Brotherhood getting closer and closer to revealing their plan to take over the earth?*

Yeah, I said. *So?*

So it sounds to me like he doesn't want regular humans to find out about his plans. Maybe getting you kicked out of school wasn't the only reason he disabled the cameras in the gym. Maybe he just didn't want any witnesses. And he spent weeks pretending to be Dr. Logan while he excavated the temple. Why would he have bothered with all that unless he really wanted to hide what he was doing from the mortal world until the time was right?

Lin was right! *I wonder what Anubis would do if some tourists should happen to poke their heads into this room right now.*

But how are we supposed to get them in here? Doli asked. There's the gate in the way, and I don't think anyone can hear us through it.

And we can't go into the main temple like this, Lin added. *We'll scare those poor people half to death.*

So we'll transform first, I answered. *And, Vishnu, can you undo the magic holding the gate together without breaking the shield, till I get out?*

He paused, and then nodded.

I don't think I can make it, Lin groaned, attempting to haul herself up but failing miserably.

I'll stay with her, Doli said firmly. *I can protect her and Vishnu when the shield is broken.*

I began to protest, but Doli cut across me. *There isn't time to argue. Come on. You never needed an excuse before to go in, all guns blazing.*

I almost laughed, and Lin raised her head defiantly. *Go. Now. Let's do this.* I focused my mind, but at first nothing happened. For a few moments I was terrified that I had been in my lion form for so long that I was trapped in feline form forever. But slowly, slowly, my claws receded and became nails. My paws gave way to my hands and sneakered feet. I breathed a sigh of relief. It felt amazing to be human. I would never take it for granted again.

As I ran forward past Anubis, Vishnu's protective shield bulged with me like a water bubble just before it pops. As I reached the gate, and the shield touched the enchanted metal, the gate immediately tumbled to the floor into tangled scraps again. The dark magic that had been holding it together had now been neutralized by Vishnu's glowing protection.

The bubble of Vishnu's protective shield then burst into a shower of shimmering raindrops as I cleared the room and ran into the main temple.

"Help! Help us! Please!" Some men wrapped in orange-and-red cloth gave me astonished looks, but I didn't think they understood me. Luckily, a group of Australian tourists who had been observing the red-and-gold statue of Ganesh came running right away, asking what was wrong.

"It's my friend, she's hurt," I said.

I pointed at the small room and waved for them to hurry. As I turned to lead the way back to the chamber, I heard a plaintive roar echoing through the hall. *What's going on in there?* I wondered. Was Anubis standing his ground, putting up a fight, or was our plan about to backfire? If he decided now was the time to reveal the Brotherhood of Chaos to the masses, then all I was doing was leading a bunch of kind strangers to their deaths. It would be a massacre!

But when I reached the room, everything was eerily quiet. The Shiva statue was back on its pedestal, cross-legged and still, as if he had never come to life. The hole in the floor had disappeared, along with the eagle corpses. And Anubis was gone. The only figures that remained were Lin, Doli, and Vishnu—who once again had only two arms. He had transformed into the kindly old tea seller I had met in the market. They were all hunched over something I couldn't see. It had to be Ana.

My hand flew to my mouth. Ana had passed out as a jaguar. If she was still a Wildcat when these tourists got to her, we would have a lot of explaining to do. But as I got closer, I saw a girl in jeans and a plain long-sleeved red T-shirt—the same one she'd been wearing the very first time I'd met her. It was Ana, and she was human again! I ran to her side, knelt down next to her, and touched her hand. Her eyes fluttered open. There was a big bump swelling on her forehead. "What . . . what's going on?" she asked. "Where's Anu—" She broke off when she saw the small crowd of tourists gathering around her, looking at her with concern.

"What happened?" one of the Australian tourists asked. "Your friend said you got hurt."

Ana stared at him. "Uh," she said after a moment. "I'm . . . so embarrassed. I fell and I, um, hit my head on the statue," she said.

"Looks like you banged it pretty good," the man said, wincing at the knot on her head.

Ana reached up and rubbed the bruised lump. "Yeah, I guess I did."

A slim blond man knelt down and took Ana's hand in his, pressing his fingers to Ana's wrist and looking at the watch on his own wrist, as if he were checking her pulse. "I'm a nurse," the man explained. "Your pulse is all right. I'd tell your mother to take you to the doctor to have your head checked out, though. You may have hit it hard enough to cause a concussion. How are you feeling?"

Ana looked at him, clearly trying to decide how to answer. But then her gaze shifted to a spot on the floor just past the nurse. She leaned forward, grabbed something at the base of the Shiva statue, and gripped it in her fist. Slowly she stood up and turned her back to the tourists so that only we could see her face. She broke into a huge smile as she opened her hand. "Actually," she said, "I'm feeling much better now."

In her palm was a glittering red gemstone. She'd found one more key that would lock the eagle Chaos Spirits in the vase for good.

chapter 19

Ana

ONCE THE EXCITEMENT WAS OVER AND THE TOURISTS had gone back to their tours, my friends and I ran to the man who'd given us the tea, and hugged him close. He laughed and hugged us back, but he remained silent. It was as if he knew that even his words contained powerful magic, not to be wasted. Either way, I knew he understood us.

"Thank you, Vishnu," I whispered. "You helped save our lives."

"How can we ever repay you?" Lin asked.

Vishnu merely bowed to us and touched his hand to his heart as if to say that our thanks was enough. He stayed behind in the chamber, watching over the statue of Shiva, looking as if he had no plans to leave anytime soon. I realized he might have been doing the same thing Ixchel had done in Cancún with Quetzalcoatl. He was making sure Shiva never got another chance to join Anubis's all-star team of destructive gods. Our thanks was nowhere near enough.

As we crossed the street, the black cat came running out of the park and fell in step with us. "You're back!" I cried. "I was worried about you."

"Well, look who decided to grace us with her presence," Shani deadpanned. "Ever noticed that she always disappears whenever we get attacked by ancient gods?"

But I didn't care about that. I was just glad she was safe. I leaned down, picked her up, and draped her over my shoulders. She purred into my ear and nuzzled against my face. "She may not be a fighter, but she's great at showing us where the action is."

Lin and Shani exchanged a look. "You mean she's really good at showing us the very best place to get ourselves killed," Shani retorted. "Why are we friends with this cat, again?"

"Because she's our mascot," I reminded her.

Shani shrugged. "Anything beats Eddie the Eagle, I guess. I swear, I'm so happy I didn't make the tennis team now. I don't think I'll ever wear anything with an eagle on it for the rest of my life."

"Me neither," Doli agreed. "I might have to propose a new mascot to Coach Connolly for the track team T-shirts. Otherwise my track career is over."

Lin reached over and scratched the cat between her ears. "I wonder if she knew we were going to get attacked by all those crazy birds, though."

"I don't know," Doli said, "but it doesn't really matter. She never leads us into anything that the four of us can't handle—with a little help. Speaking of which, Ana, are you really okay?"

I thought for a moment. "I really am, actually." I reached my hand up to my forehead and felt the bump there—it was already getting smaller. "I think that tea Vishnu gave us protected us from the worst of our injuries. If it hadn't been for him, I'm not sure we would've made it." I glanced at Shani, who was walking on my left, and stopped in my tracks. "Oh my God, Shani, your ear!"

She smirked. "What about it? Did it fall off altogether?"

"No," I said in wonder. "It's healed!"

Shani stopped walking and reached up to touch her wound. The tear that had been there was gone, the two halves reunited as if they'd never been apart. Shani faced me, her eyes watering. "I have my ear back," she said in a shaky voice. "It must have been the tea."

I furrowed my brows. "If I didn't know you better, I'd think you were about to cry. Are you all right?"

Shani bit her lip and scratched at her arm, as if she were allergic to her own emotions. "I just . . . I want to thank you, Ana, for pushing me out of the way and going after Anubis. You didn't have to do that. I swear I would have done it." She swallowed hard, her dark eyes searching mine.

I reached out and squeezed her shoulder. "I know that," I said, giving her a small smile. "That's exactly why I didn't want you to. You're so smart and loyal—we couldn't risk losing you.

Besides, you've already sacrificed so much, things you can never get back."

"Don't you go thinking I've sacrificed my school just yet," she said, pointing her finger at me with a determined look in her eye. "Principal Ferris said she might let me back into Temple."

"I was talking about your hair," I said with a wink.

Shani smiled and pulled me into a tight hug.

"All right, you two. How about we save the mushy stuff for later, huh?" Lin said. "We should get back to the jet and see if we can get in touch with Ms. Benitez."

"The jet?" Shani said, her eyes bulging.

I nodded. "Principal Ferris thinks we took it to Cancún for a research project."

"Wow," she said. "I wish I could go with you guys. But I should get home. My dad's probably going crazy looking for me by now."

I exchanged a nervous look with Lin and Doli. "Shani, about your dad . . ." I started. I explained what had happened at her father's apartment—how her dad didn't seem to remember who she or her sisters were. For a second her face blanched and something tender passed across her face. "He doesn't remember me?"

I shook my head. "There was no trace of you at the apartment. It was weird."

Shani furrowed her brows. "That *is* weird." Then she gave

me a sly smile. "But you say he doesn't remember my sisters either, huh? Well, at least that's something."

"There is one more thing," I continued. I told her that I had seen Kiah transform into a dog.

"I knew it!" Shani cried. "I knew there was something fishy about that little creep." She punched one fist into her hand. "Well, it looks like Anubis has sort of hijacked my life here, which means I'm coming with you guys . . . if you'll have me."

"Are you kidding? Of course we'll have you!" Doli exclaimed. "We'll figure out what to do after we get Ms. Benitez to help us free your dad from Anubis's magic."

"And to find my aunt and uncle," I added. "I know we won just now, but we still have two more gemstones to find and two more Chaos Spirits to defeat."

"Not to mention that Anubis is still out there, and we know he's looking for a new friend. Even if Vishnu holds Shiva in the temple, we don't know what's going to happen with Quetzal-coatl, if Ms. Benitez wasn't able to finish the ritual she told us about," Lin added.

Shani sighed. "Anubis isn't going to give up if those two don't work out either. So the Brotherhood is growing. A Wildcat's work is never done, huh?"

I shook my head. "Not yet, anyway. But at least we've got each other."

Doli nodded. "Wildcats stick together."

We piled our hands on top of one another's and then let them fly apart.

"Let's get back to the airport," I said. "We'll take it from there."

We started walking around the edge of the park in search of a busy street where we could catch a taxi. As we walked, it sank in for me how easily any of us could have died over the past couple of days. I knew it was a weird time to think of Jason, but I couldn't help it. There was so much left unsaid between us. I would have really hated it if we left things the way they were. True, he had asked for time, but I was sure he would at least want to know that we were in one piece after fighting off three different ancient gods. I pulled my phone out of my jeans pocket and typed out a quick text.

In Mumbai—seriously scary stuff here! Huge battle, but we made it out alive. See you soon, I hope.

While the others drifted into the now empty street, talking about what we would do once we got back to the jet, I fell silent on the sidewalk, thinking of Jason and how he'd smiled at me that day when he had waited for me after morning assembly. After a few minutes of walking, my phone dinged. I looked down and quickly read Jason's text back.

Good for you. Glad ur OK, but I think we're done, Ana. Sorry.

My breath rushed out of me in a whoosh. *He can't be serious.* I couldn't believe it. I just kept staring at the screen, hoping the letters would rearrange themselves into words that made sense. But then I felt my foot catch on something, and before I knew it, I was going down. "Aaaaahhh!"

I saw it all in slow motion. On the way down, the black cat, who had been perched on my shoulders, leaped off and landed gracefully on her dainty paws. I wasn't nearly as suave. I broke my fall with my hands, scraping them on the pavement and landing with an *oof*.

"Whoa! Are you okay, Ana?" Doli called, heading my way.

"I think so," I said, turning over to find out what it was I'd tripped over. At first, in the darkness of the evening, it looked like a pile of clothes. Then the pile groaned, and I realized it was a human body! I gasped, then scrambled to the person and turned him over. Maybe the man had had a heart attack or something and needed help. "Sir?" I said breathlessly. "Sir, are you all right?"

When he didn't answer, Doli said, "Pull back his hood; make sure he's breathing." I did, but when I saw the man's face, I was the one who stopped breathing.

"Uncle Mec!" I collapsed over him, hugging him with all my might. "I can't believe it! What are you doing here?"

He didn't respond. *He must be hurt,* I thought with rising panic. I eased him back onto the ground while Doli whipped off the light jacket she was wearing, rolled it into a ball, and tucked it under Uncle Mec's head. "It's so dark," I complained. "I can't see what's wrong with him."

Shani snapped her fingers and said, "Somebody give me a

phone." Doli pulled hers out and handed it to her without hesitation. Shani tapped a few buttons, and suddenly the phone became a beacon of light. "It's a high-powered flashlight app," she explained. She handed me the phone.

I held it up to light my uncle's face. His lip was bloodied and his cheeks were battered and bruised. He looked like he had been hit by a bus. And he wasn't moving. Was he breathing? I couldn't tell. "Uncle Mec!" I yelled, shaking him gently. "Please, please wake up."

Finally he eased one eye open and looked at me. "Ana?" he croaked.

I breathed out in relief. He was alive. "Yes! It's me, *Tio*. What happened to you?"

"Your aunt and I—we were kidnapped."

I clamped a hand over my mouth.

"Wow, you were right all along," Lin said.

Shani kneeled down on the other side of him. "Who kidnapped you, Mr. Navarro?" she asked.

He shook his head. "I don't know. They were wearing masks."

"When did it happen?" Doli pressed.

"Right after Ana left for Temple Academy," he said. He turned his head so he could look at me. "We were so sad after we dropped you off at the airport, *niña*, we decided to go see a movie—something to cheer us up. But when we got home, the door was open. We should have called the police, but we went in anyway. Inside there were a bunch of people in animal masks. They threw black sacks over our heads and ushered us into a van parked out back. After that, they kept us blindfolded and moving around a lot. They told us we should behave ourselves or we might never see you again."

I had to choke back a sob. It explained so much. That had been the reason that they'd never checked on me. They'd been prisoners all this time.

"They brought us to a room somewhere—I don't know where. Every once in a while they would move us—into a car, onto a plane, into another room, but we were always blindfolded. I never got to see who was keeping us prisoner or where they were taking us. We never got to talk to anyone but each other."

"But—but Aunt Teppy called me," I said, tears running down my face now. "She told me to leave you guys alone, not to come looking for you. She said you'd gone to Cancún on vacation."

Uncle Mec looked confused. "No, Ana, Teppy never called you. They wouldn't let us use a phone. And we wouldn't go anywhere without telling you first. You know that. But we thought about you every minute. And Aunt Teppy prayed for you every night. She probably still is."

I felt a hand on my shoulder, and turned to see Shani looking at me with compassion in her eyes. "It must have been Nicole, Ana," she said. "We suspected that anyway."

I couldn't help it. I broke down in painful sobs. On the one hand, I felt relief—my aunt and uncle *did* love me, and I was right to have believed that the phone calls had just been another trick of an evil being. But I also felt horror, because now I knew for sure that Aunt Teppy was being held hostage and it was all my fault. "Why did they let you go?" I asked.

"To send you a message," he said. "They wanted me to tell you and your friends to stop fighting them, or else . . ."

I stared at him in shock. He knew we were Hunters. "Or else what?" I pressed.

"Ana," he said, his own eyes tearing up. "They still have your aunt. And they said if you don't stay out of their way, there will be more victims. . . ."

"More victims?"

But the shrill sound of Taylor Swift singing "Bad Blood" sounded from Lin's pocket. Lin, who had been watching the scene between my uncle and me in fascinated silence, widened her eyes. "Sorry!" she cried.

She pulled out her phone from her back pocket. "Hello?" As she listened, all the color drained from her face. "What do you mean, Dad? No . . ." She lowered her hand and let her phone clatter to the ground.

Shani picked up the phone and stared at her. "Lin, what is it?"

"That was my dad calling from Shanghai," she said, her eyes staring blindly ahead. "My mother is missing!"

ACKNOWLEDGMENTS

ONCE AGAIN, THIS SERIES IS A TEAM EFFORT, WHICH MEANS I have many people to thank.

First, a *huge* thank-you to Fiona Simpson, my editor at Simon & Schuster, and to Brendan Duffy, Stephanie Lane Elliott, William Severs, and Ali Standish. How lucky am I to have access to such smart, creative people who are always full of good ideas and great advice? Thank you all so much! You're the greatest, I hope you know.

Thank you to the whole team at Aladdin, including Laura Lyn DiSiena, Kayley Hoffman, Shifa Kapadwala, Kara Reilly, Sarah Kwak, and everyone in sales, marketing, and promotion. And of course immense gratitude to Wylie Beckert for creating yet another incredible cover. (Whenever I do school events, the kids ask me if I designed the cover. I always have to say no and that they should be glad I didn't—unless they're really into stick figures.) Thank you to Diane Derroches and the organizers of Simon & Schuster's celebration of Latino Heritage Month. It was an honor to be included, to meet the group of high school seniors who participated, and to share my love of books and writing with them. Thank you to Jeannie Ng for introducing me to the wonderful world of Simon & Schuster Children's Books in the first place.

Thank you to a very important group of people: the readers! Thank you so much for taking the time to read my books, and for reading in general. It's still surreal for me that anyone outside of my immediate family has read anything I've written. So it's a treat when someone who lives on the other side of the country (like my new friend Kira Nguyen) reaches out to share her thoughts about the book. I am in awe of all the kids I've met in person (Hi, kids from the Queens Library in Corona and P.S. 33Q!) and online. Your enthusiasm about books and stories and imagination makes me so happy and hopeful for the future. Keep it up!

Thank you to the group of writers and librarians I met at the BooksNJ festival: Tracey Baptiste, Selene Castrovilla, Margaret Gelbwasser, Sharon Kalman, and Arlene Sahraie. It's so cool to meet such a fun, driven, and intelligent group of women who are making a go of this writing thing, or who are doing everything in their power to keep libraries alive and well.

I've had a lot of friends from high school invite me to their kids' schools, offer me writing opportunities, send me pictures of their kids reading my books, or attend my author events that I just have to give a shout-out to my alma mater: Stuyvesant High School. Thank you, class of '93, for being my friends back then and for still having my back all these years later. I love you guys! Thanks also to my Penn State friends for all the support now, and for being wise critics in our writing workshops way back when. Thank you to my friends at Penguin Random House for keeping me sane and making me laugh during my years as a production editor when I was trying to juggle work, writing, and freelancing. I'm in your debt for reminding me to have a life and for being part of it! Thank you to my new coworkers/friends at Working Partners Ltd. for making me feel like I was part of the team all along.

And finally, to my family, especially Mom and Dad—and to my friends who might as well be family—thank you for all the love you've given me, for being my biggest fans no matter what, and for forgiving me when I have a writing deadline and have to ignore you for a while. I don't know what I would do without you.

Crystal Velasquez is the author of *Hunters of Chaos*, the Your Life, but . . . series: *Your Life, but Better*; *Your Life, but Cooler*; and *Your Life, but Sweeter*; and four books in the Maya & Miguel series, based on the television show—*My Twin Brother/My Twin Sister*; *Neighborhood Friends*; *The Valentine Machine*; and *Paint the Town*. She holds a BA in creative writing from Penn State University and is a graduate of NYU's Summer Publishing Institute. Currently an editor at Working Partners Ltd. and a freelance proofreader, she lives in Flushing, Queens. Visit Crystal's website at crystalvelasquez.com, visit her blog at yourlifebutbetter.blogspot.com, or find her on Facebook at Facebook.com/CrystalVelasquezAuthor.